Ghosts of Texas

Trail to Black Coulee, Volume 1

Tommie Wendall

Published by Tommie Wendall, 2021.

GHOSTS OF TEXAS

First edition. April 30, 2021.

Copyright © 2021 Tommie Wendall.

ISBN: 979-8201494216

Written by Tommie Wendall.

Table of Contents

To the people we meet along the way.

Texas

1867

The storm lurked in the overcast sky most of the day. When it broke, the rain burst from black clouds and pounded into the hard ground. Lightning split the growing darkness and thunder cut deep into the heart of the solitary figure that followed a carriage trail through the oak dotted landscape.

His gray coat, worn and stained, hung from his thin frame like sackcloth. Pulling up the collar, he held it shut with his left hand, tucking his right across his body. The thunder brought him shivers, not the cold, and he fought the instinct to crawl into a hole or a ditch and hide. He could now with no one present to call him a coward or a deserter. Though fear ran often and thick in his blood, he decided long ago it was easier to cut it off from his mind and move forward, ever forward until someone called a retreat.

Now, he advanced through the storm, hoping for a dry place to sleep. He spent so many nights in the rain over the last few years with no blanket and no fire that he refused to spend another if he had a choice.

Ahead lay a hacienda. That much he learned in town before the shopkeeper expelled him from the store with a well-aimed boom handle. The knot in his scalp still throbbed as he trudged through the darkness, silently praying the thunder would quit.

As the hours passed, the storm faded into the east, and the rain eased to a drizzle. When the dark shadows of the hacienda rose into view from the muddy grassland, the drizzle, too, ceased falling. Tired, hungry, and now shivering from a bone-deep chill, the wanderer pushed on.

Nothing moved around the place. He paused outside the gate anyway, still cautious of buildings and places where riflemen might hide. Fighting down the fear of ambush, he stepped through the gate and crossed the open distance to the front door, knocked and waited. Minutes passed while he nervously watched the yard.

The door opened, and a girl peered out at him through the narrow crack. "*Si?*"

"Is Señor Alvarado home?"

"*Si.*" The girl nodded once. With a measuring glance, she took in his appearance and all it said of him. "What is your business with him?" she asked in a guarded tone.

He hesitated, knowing that for all her youth, this girl could slam the door in his face and leave him to freeze on the open land. He felt awkward and light-headed with anxiety.

"I have some questions," he told her. "Private questions."

Her eyes narrowed. Then a male voice spoke in Spanish from the fire lit room beyond the door. The girl replied over her shoulder and frowned at what the man said in return. Then she stepped back, opening the door to admit him with a sharp wave of her hand.

Removing his hat, he crossed the threshold into the warm foyer. The man, a Spaniard from the cut of his coat and trousers, stood in the arched doorway to the right, silhouetted by firelight. He spoke what sounded like a command, gesturing the drenched wanderer closer. Once tall, his shoulders now hunched beneath the black coat, resembling a perched vulture. As the wanderer moved closer, he could make out the Spaniard's face, weather scarred like the arid land beyond the walls of the hacienda.

The Spaniard regarded him with the same suspicion as the girl at the door. Without a doubt, this was Señor Alvarado from the regal lift of his chin. After a long, silent scrutiny, he asked a question that the wanderer did not understand though the words teased at a long dormant part of his knowledge. When he failed to reply, the obsidian black eyes narrowed.

"Your name?" Alvarado asked with a thin vein of impatience in his tone.

"Martin," the wanderer replied.

Alvarado's frown deepened. "And your family name?"

To this, Martin could only lower his gaze in embarrassment.

The old man blinked and spoke in clear, stern English. "Did your mother not teach you it is rude to not answer when an elder asks a question?"

Martin nodded and responded politely. "She also told me it is better to remain silent than tell a lie."

Alvarado's expression remained stern a moment longer before giving way to a mirthless smile. He turned away and moved toward the firelight. Two strides away, he stopped and turned back.

"Come, *Martín*," he said, giving the name a Spanish inflection as he waved a hand toward the sitting room beyond the entryway. "No guest is denied here."

"Sir, I don't wish to impose on your hospitality," Martin said. "I only wish to ask questions."

"What kind of questions?"

Martin swallowed and reached inside himself to open up a part of him that had lain locked away for nearly ten years.

"About my mother, sir. I understand she may have grown up here."

If there had been any friendliness in Alvarado's face, it vanished. "And, your mother's name?"

"Maitea. I don't know her last name."

Alvarado's mouth hardened and he turned away quickly. "Come sit by the fire. My bones ache with cold."

With no other choice, Martin followed the Spaniard deeper into the room where firelight played over thick adobe walls. A faded rug covered the floor beneath red satin furniture. Alvarado settled into a high-backed chair near the fire. Martin sank to the hearth facing him, thankful for the abundant warmth.

"Lolita," Alvarado called. When the girl appeared in the doorway, he told her to bring food and warm wine.

Martin felt a spark of excitement when the words formed meaning in his mind. He extended his hands to the fire but drew back as the heat seemed to sear his chilled flesh.

"These spring rains chill to the bones, and you've come far from the look of those shoes."

They could hardly be called shoes anymore. Holes in the souls left his bare feet exposed as did tears in the knees of his trousers and elbows of his shirt. Only the old gray coat seemed fit for use any longer.

Alvarado took up a long stemmed pipe from the table beside him. He bent forward, lit a long splinter in the fire, and held it to the bowl. He sat back and puffed quietly for a long while.

"Tell me about your mother," the Spaniard said at length. "What did she look like?"

Martin closed his eyes, summoning the memory. Though his mother's features remained vivid in his mind, kept alive by the picture he carried with him, her living image had faded.

"She was delicate in form, golden-brown hair, and green eyes."

"And her character?"

"Gentle and kind, always willing to sacrifice for those in need."

Alvarado frowned in thought. "Did she tell you anything else about your family?"

"She talked about my grandfather and her brother a little."

"And your father? What of him?"

Martin glanced into the firelight. "She did only..."

"Only what?"

Martin swallowed, a twist of sadness forming in his throat. "He was killed by Indians up in Kansas."

Alvarado's head cocked in curiosity. "And so your grandfather and uncle are your last hope of finding a family?"

"Yes, sir."

Alvarado gave a slow nod. "I see. What do you know of them?"

Martin looked down at his hands as the memory of his mother's dying words came to him. "My mother only referred to them by their first names, but she mentioned this ranch, warning me never to come here."

"What makes you think they live here?" Alvarado took a deep draw on his pipe, and Martin watched his face through the smoke.

"I don't know," he said with a shrug. "I figured there were ties here."

"Their names? Your grandfather and uncle?"

"She called them just *Abuelo* and *Tío*. She never told me their names."

Again, Alvarado descended into thought. Martin waited anxiously, hoping the old man would remember something. He searched the old man's face but saw no signs of recollection. Hopelessness nagged at the back of his mind until he turned toward the fire and extended his hands again. This time he could tolerated the sting of his warming flesh.

"How long ago did your mother leave?" Alvarado asked.

"Almost twenty years ago." Martin paused. "I was too young to remember it clearly, but I remember some."

"What do you remember?"

Martin glanced over the room again, taking in the heavy Spanish influence in the decoration and finding it soothing. He hesitated to explain for fear his heritage might cause the old man to expel him into the cold night. Drawing a deep breath, he resigned himself to the fate of another cold night.

"My father was an American. I believe my grandmother did not approve of his marriage to my mother. After my father was killed, I believe my mother left to avoid a forced marriage. That's all I know."

Alvarado stared down into the bowl of his pipe and shook his head. "I apologize, but your story is unfamiliar to me. I do not recall such a thing happening to any of the families on my *hacienda*."

Martin swallowed his disappointment as once again his inquiries met a dead-end. He gazed into the fire, trying to think what to do next.

"However, if you require work, that I can give you."

Again, Martin studied the man through the smoke. He was not unpleasant, but something remained strange about him. Regardless of his sense of this man, Martin needed a job. For the last three months, he had walked with only the clothes on his back and lived on the food kind souls gave out of pity. With this dead end in front of him, there was no use in pushing on any longer.

"How are you with horses?" Alvarado asked.

"I've only ridden a couple of times, and those were sway-backed nags."

"Well, when Armand's done with you, you'll know them well enough." Alvarado rose and gestured Martin toward the door. "Lolita can show you to the men's bunk room. You'll find her in the kitchen just down the hall from the front door." He sank back into his chair and his attention turned inward, giving Martin the sense that the conversation was over.

Martin rose from the hearth and bowed at the shoulders the way his mother taught him. "Thank you, sir."

Alvarado waved his hand dismissively, and Martin retreated to the foyer. Away from the fire's warmth, he shivered, but he hoped the young woman, Lolita, might have a lit stove in the kitchen. He walked down the hall, listening for sounds of movement.

Lolita nearly collided with him as he stepped through the door. He caught the decanter before she dropped it and her arm before she fell from the step. She jerked free.

"I thought you'd be in Señor Luis's company a little longer," she said eyes wide in irritation. She turned away going to the table and setting the plate down.

"It seems he's given me a job." Martin moved to the cook stove. He reached toward it and felt residual heat radiating off the metal. "Have you a water bucket?"

She scoffed. "Why don't you wring it out of your clothes if you want water?"

Her words hurt. Like the stones they'd cast at him in Port Arthur and Houston, they made it plain he was unwelcome. He turned his back to her and reached his hands toward the stove in defiance of her anger.

She stood silent for a long moment. When she spoke again, her tone softened.

"We have water here." She filled a glass and brought it to him. As he drank she reached out and felt his coat, then without pretense she slipped her hand inside the open collar to feel his shirt. "You are soaked!" She spun around, twirling her long black hair in a wide arc that brushed his chest. She was younger than him but carried herself with the confidence of womanhood. "Stay here, I will get you dry clothes."

Taking the plate and the water, he sat beside the stove and ate. The first few bites knotted his stomach and so he ate little.

When Lolita returned, she had a cotton shirt and trousers which she handed over to him. She nodded toward the pantry. "In there, you can change. Leave that cloak on the stove to dry."

He obeyed. The clothes fit loosely and were short in the sleeves and pant legs. The wide belt required a new hole which he cut with a pocket knife, a tricky thing to do in the thick darkness of the pantry. When he stepped out, Lolita looked him over and pursed her lips.

"They'll do," she said.

"Whose are they?"

"None of your business." She took his bundle of wet clothes. "I'll wash these. They smell."

"I've been wearing them for the last five years and then some." He returned to his place by the stove, aware that she studied him.

"At least you're still alive to talk about it," she muttered.

He ignored her and continued eating. "Señor Luis said you can show me where to bed for the night."

"Go to hell."

Martin turned a frown on her. "I didn't mean it that way, ma'am. I meant, could you show me where the bunkhouse is?"

Her expression softened. "Straight across the yard out that door. Be quiet. The men will be asleep by now. They don't like being disturbed in their sleep." With that warning, she disappeared through the side door, the latch clicking loudly.

Martin pondered over her while he finished his food. Then his thoughts turned to his own situation and forgot her tantrums while he waited for the fire to drive away the last of the chill.

The bunkhouse overflowed with the scent of unwashed men sweating in the heat of an over built fire. Even with the thin glow from the stove, finding an empty bed proved dangerous. As Martin crept between the bunks, he brushed a blanket draped over an outstretched arm. Suddenly, the blanket flew back, slapping him in the face and a solid force struck him in the chest, knocking him against the wall and forcing the air from his lungs. The cold edge of a knife pressed against his throat.

"Last words?" The man's breath was foul and his voice grating. Martin nearly gagged.

"Just looking for a bed," Martin said. "Didn't mean to wake you, mister."

In the dim light from the dying fire, the man's sparkling eyes narrowed. The shadows deepened the lines of his face. With a jerk and a shove, he threw Martin to the floor and stood over him.

"The top on the end is open." He hauled back and kicked Martin in the gut, causing Martin's stomach to tighten around the food he had eaten. "Just don't sleep too deep." He returned to his bed amid the chuckles of the other men who roused enough to watch the brief conflict.

Taking shallow breaths, Martin carefully rolled to his knees and used the wall to stand. Men rolled over or settled deeper into their blankets and paid him no mind. Even the man on the bed beneath the empty one turned his back to Martin and pulled his blankets over his head.

The bunk had no blankets. He glanced at the fireplace and decided to sleep in a warmer spot. Even the old gray coat would keep him warm by a fire.

The coals danced with thin threads of light as he added a couple more lengths of wood and slid down against the wall, folding like a pocketknife with his knees against his chest. He wrapped the coat about his legs and buttoned it, remembering the man who gave it to him so many years before. That man had been the closest thing to a brother Martin knew and died saving his life in the last days of the war, leaving Martin with only memories both comforting and saddening. His death served as the impetus for Martin's journey here, the spark lighting hope that his family still lived.

Tonight, that hope died with Luis Alvarado's certainty that no one like his mother, uncle, or grandfather lived here. Still, Martin could not believe his mother created the stories to quiet his anxious search for identity as a boy. In those days, he never could have understood her reasoning, or her stories and the people in them, but now that he could, the truth eluded him. This puzzled, frightened and agitated him until his mind, exhausted by emotion and thought, surrendered to sleep.

He dozed until sunlight grayed the windows and a rooster crowed. Martin woke at the first sound of movement. A man rolled out of his bunk, pulled on his boots and coat, and walked out into the morning twilight in a groggy half-stagger. He seemed unaware of Martin's presence as he nearly tripped over him.

Martin debated staying beside the dying coals or getting more wood. The night had been long and unsettling, and the last thing he wanted was more trouble.

Taking the poker he stirred the coals and added a few more logs before going outside.

The air was fresh and cool. As he stood on the narrow porch watching the chickens, the door opened.

"Sleep good?"

He recognized the voice and refused to turn or respond as the man closed the door and came to stand close beside him.

"Grayback, eh?" The man chuckled showing rotted teeth. "Well don't that beat all."

Martin shifted his gaze from the chickens to the corral where a handful of horses stood dozing.

"I heard you boys tucked tail and run after Richmond. Figure that's why we lost the war." He stuck his face to within inches of Martin's. "That true, soldier boy?"

Martin glanced down, watching the man's hands out of the corner of his eye, but said nothing. His heartbeat slowed. In a surly morning mood like this, he welcomed a fight but his weariness tempered the desire.

"Maybe I should put my knife to your throat again. Maybe then you'll talk."

Taking a slow breath, Martin looked up into the man's eyes and waited. The man's grin faltered, his left eye twitching uneasily. He backed off a step and stood there, his right hand resting against the holster strapped over his long underwear. Unarmed, Martin stood no chance against the man and did not care. Martin turned his back and stepped off the porch wandering toward the corral. He heard the door open again followed by quiet conversation.

Putting the indiscernible whispers from his mind, he leaned against the fence and watched the horses as they woke and went about their own morning routine. Lost in thought, the jingle of spurs startled him. He looked up to see a man in a broad Mexican hat and tall boots approach.

"You Martin?"

He nodded.

"I'm Armand. I run this ranch for Señor Luis. I understand he hired you last night."

"Yes, sir."

Armand looked him over. "You've seen more hard times than hard work." Martin held the man's gaze as Armand studied him. "Can you use a gun?"

"I can."

Armand's eyes narrowed. He smiled. "You must be good to answer like that. No emotion. The ones that cannot make it sound more important."

Martin felt the hair on his neck stand up.

"Señor Luis said I'd be working with horses."

"For now." Armand considered him a moment longer before he turned away toward the kitchen. "You'll miss breakfast if you stand there much longer."

Martin's stomach rumbled and he followed at a quick walk.

Nearly twenty men crowded the long table in the center of the room. All devoured the food in the ravenous manner of hogs. It reminded him of a time a few months after Gettysburg when his company devoured all the food they found at a homestead. His hand went to the scar, hidden above his temple, a reminder of that day.

"Dig in," Armand ordered as he took the only chair at the head of the table.

Martin skirted the table, searching for a break in the wall of men. Across the table, Lolita cast him a glance that showed both worry and anger. He found a gap between two men and squeezed in, gathering what he could onto his plate. The pickings were already slim, but he got enough to satiate his hunger. As he reached out for the last biscuit, he barely avoided the blade of the toothless man a second time. The point of the knife split the plate and bit deep into the tabletop. Stillness descended on the room. Martin ignored it. He split the biscuit and sandwiched a slice of bacon between the halves.

"Pretty fast hands," the man purred. "Bet you're pretty good with a gun or fancy yourself that way, eh, gray boy?"

"Lay off him, Kell," Armand said with little force.

The toothless man, Kell, glanced over at the boss.

"He ain't nothing but a skinny little rat, hardly even worth carving."

"Then get that knife out of the table and finish your meal," Armand ordered.

Kell's upper lip twitched in a sneer. He jerked the knife free and, with a facial shrug, went back to shoveling eggs into his mouth.

Martin went on eating. He was the last to leave the table. Armand waited for him on the porch.

"You'll start out in the stables, cleaning." He fixed Martin with a knowing look. "You ever shovel shit before?"

"I've done my share."

"Well, you're going to do more." Armand waved a hand for Martin to follow and led him to the barn, where he pointed out a rake, shovel, and wheelbarrow. "When you're done cleaning out stalls, clean the tack room. It hasn't been done all winter." He left it at that, with Martin staring at his back as he crossed the yard. As he passed the kitchen, Lolita threw a dishpan full of water from the door, nearly hitting him. Both froze, staring at each other. Then Armand started for her and she retreated inside, bolting the door.

Martin bit his lip. It was none of his business.

Shedding the old gray coat, he hung it on a peg in the tack room and went to work in the stalls. It took most of the morning, but he finished before lunch and started cleaning the tack room.

The weeks that followed he found contentment with the work, for the menial nature of the work caused the other hands to leave him alone. Even Kell had nothing to do with him. The nights however, left him restless. Having no blankets, he slept in his coat, but good food kept him warm. Then one evening, he found an old quilt on his bunk. It was threadbare, but it was something. As he fingered the tattered edge of a patch cut from the same cloth as the borrowed shirt, he smiled, knowing where the gift came from. But even Lolita's kindness could not ease his mind when it came to the threats of the men.

A month passed and payday came. Martin was grooming one of Señor Luis's favorite mares when Armand brought him his time.

"Will you be moving on now?" Armand asked.

Martin shook his head. "I'd like to work off a horse and saddle. First, I need boots and a few other things."

Armand nodded, glancing over the shirt and trousers Martin was gradually filling out.

"Lolita needs supplies. She's leaving tomorrow morning. You can drive the wagon."

"Thanks." Martin pocketed the coins and turned back to his work.

"Just don't get any ideas about her," Armand said suddenly. "Lolita's my woman."

Martin looked at him, wondering if the man could be serious. Armand looked away first and walked out of the barn.

The next morning, in the gray dawn, Martin hitched the team and pulled the wagon around to the kitchen as Lolita walked out. She frowned and started climbing to the seat before Martin had a chance to offer help. When he extended his hand, she ignored it and perched on the edge of the seat, putting as much distance between them as she could. He stared at her in a silent question, and she glared at him.

"Drive, *puta*!"

He understood her insult, but not her motive. He clucked to the team, and they started down the road in enduring silence. An hour passed before Martin worked up the courage to speak.

"I want to thank you for the blanket," he said.

Lolita scoffed. "It was the dog's before she died."

A smile, quiet and brief, flashed across Martin's face. "Reckon that's fitting the way folks been treating me." He glanced over at her, and she looked away. Martin let the silence hang for a while, but gradually, the burning agitation in her wore on him.

"What you got against me, señorita?"

Her hard expression faltered. She crossed her arms and lifted her chin, refusing to answer.

"I know you don't have much cause to be partial to me. I'd just like to say 'hello' to you in the morning and you say 'hello' back like you do the other men."

Her eyes were wide and soft as she stared at him. Then she stared at the horses for a long while before answering.

"You're decent. That's what I have against you." She waved a hand, encompassing the world in general. "No one's called me 'ma'am' the way you do. It's always Lolita or *puta* or *perra*." Her lips pressed hard together as she met his gaze. "You don't belong with them. Yes, men can be rough, but these..." She shook her head. "Have you heard of the Nueces Strip?"

Martin shook his head. "Can't say I have."

"It's a hideout. Miles upon miles of country infested with Comanches and outlaws. Most of the men who work for Señor Luis lived there, *thrived* there. They're men you have no business working with. Especially here."

"Why is it Señor Luis has outlaws working for him?"

"Because of the trouble with the Terraza family west of here. Their land shares a border and they've been feuding since the time the old men courted Señorita Carmelita de Barcelona y Lopez. Señor Luis and Santiago fought to win her affections. In the end, she chose Santiago, and it was a curse on him. She was beautiful but crazy. Santiago was left fighting her at home and Señor Luis on the land. Señor Luis has sworn to kill everyone bearing the Terraza name and ordered his men to kill any rider who works for them on sight. Once they let you out of the barn, they'll expect you to kill men, no matter the circumstance."

Martin scoffed. "I doubt they'll ever let me away from the hacienda. Seems if I work there much longer, I'll turn into another pile of manure. Surprised I haven't already."

Lolita shook her head, her mouth tight as a laugh threatened to break free of her. Martin glanced over at her with his eyebrows raised in mock concern, and the laughter burst forth. She never gave in to mirth, and it took her a while to recover. At last, gasping for breath, she sobered, and then her expression became grim as she regarded him. "You have no place here. It will end all that is good in you."

"If there is any good left."

"What makes you say that?" She fixed him with that hard stare of hers that challenged him to defy her. He found it entertaining, even comical, that she thought so much about him after the names she had called him, but answering her question sobered him. He stared straight ahead.

"I don't much care to talk about it."

"Is it really that bad or do you only think it that bad?" she challenged.

It came back to him clearly, the two men he killed in the act of surrender. The woman he shot, mistaking her for a Yankee sharpshooter. The four sentries he killed for their weapons and ammunition. Part of him regretted these, though his rational mind knew what he had done had been for survival.

Unable to find the words to explain, Martin looked up into Lolita's face. Her eyes widened in fear, and he realized his expression betrayed him. She looked away, shaking her head.

"I will not ask again," she promised.

He silently thanked her.

A new, friendlier silence filled the air between them until they reached town. As Martin stopped the team in front of the dry goods store, Lolita pointed out the clothing shop.

"That's where you go. Be back in two hours." With that, she climbed down from the wagon and disappeared into the store with a flick of her braided hair.

With a pocket full of money and the Alvarado hands miles away, Martin felt drawn to relax. Ten dollars was more than he ever had at one time before in his life. He crossed the street to the shop and bought an outfit, not fancy, but new and clean. A dark-gray shirt and tan trousers, a vest and boots and he felt like a new man. He bought a hat on credit and saved seventy-five cents for a drink or two. The new clothes felt odd, and he worried they would attract attention, but he had earned a drink, and so he walked down the street to a saloon that looked vacant compared to the others.

He walked to the bar and leaned on it, waiting patiently for the bartender. He ordered a beer, and when it came, it was luxuriously cold. As he took the first sip, he noticed a handful of men studying him from the corner table. He lowered his head and tried to think of where he might have seen them before.

They spoke softly, then were silent, and Martin went on drinking. When they pushed back their chairs and crossed the room to his end of the bar, cornering Martin in the back of the saloon, he felt tension rise between his shoulder blades.

"Didn't you ride in with that cook from Alvarado's rancho?" the first asked. He was a Texan, tall and broad, with forearms of corded muscle. If Martin stood straight, his forehead would come to the man's nose. The other two were a little smaller. The Mexican fiddled with a quirt. The third had a nose kinked by too many fights. Martin studied them openly, then took another swallow from his mug.

"What of it?" he asked neutrally.

"We don't like your kind in here."

"Now, Bucho," the bartender said, his voice trembling faintly. "I don't want any trouble in here."

"I'm not making trouble." The big Texan looked down his nose at Martin. "I'm just kicking some out."

The other two took the queue to close in. Martin straightened and nearly laughed at his reflex. He managed a smile, as tension from the past month begged for him to let loose, and slowly raised his hands, palms out.

"Gentlemen, please," he said. "I just wanted to enjoy a quiet drink. Now, if you'll let me finish, I'll leave, and I won't come back."

The Texan grabbed his glass and guzzled what remained. Then he smashed the glass on the edge of the bar top.

"You're done," he said. "Now try to leave."

Martin glanced at the other two and shrugged. "I'm guessing you boys make better fences than gates."

"Are you insulting us?" the Texan challenged.

Martin smirked and shook his head. After dodging the Alvarado hands and their violent pranks, the last thing he wanted was a fight, but it also brought an itch to his knuckles and an urge to inflict a little pain.

"Mister, trouble followed me from Pennsylvania to Louisiana. Blue-coated trouble, you three ain't nothin' compared to."

The Texan's eyes narrowed. He started forward, raising his right fist.

Martin ducked under the first swing, slugged the Texan just below the rib cage, and brought his elbow back into the crooked nose of the third man. The Mexican charged, and Martin dodged him, snatched the gun from the Mexican's holster, and shoved him into the Texan. He cocked the gun, bringing the Mexican and the Texan up short. Crooked Nose staggered backward and sat down hard, blinded by blood and pain.

Suddenly, the Texan grinned as he straightened slowly.

"Now what, whelp? You walk out and we'll just come after you."

"Put your guns on the counter, belts and all," Martin ordered, hoping disarming the two men would take a little starch out of their backbones.

Crooked Nose growled and looked to the Texan who glared at Martin.

"I ain't got all day, boys," Martin said. He glanced beyond Crooked Nose, making sure no one sat against the wall. Then he snapped a shot off at the empty shot glass sitting on the table beside the man's shoulder. Shards exploded from it, and Crooked Nose, hands bloody, fumbled with the buckle of his gun belt. He threw it at Martin's feet.

"You too, big man."

The Texan held his ground, lifting his chin defiantly. Martin raised the revolver to eye level and sighted over it straight into the Texan's right eye. That was enough to break the Texan's nerve. Reaching down with his left hand, the Texan unbuckled his gun belt and tossed it beside the other.

"Now, I would like you to pay for that half beer you took."

"I ain't got the money."

"Well, ain't that a shame," Martin drawled. "Maybe I should take it out on your knees." He lowered the gun as though to aim, but stepped in and kicked the man instead just below the kneecap. The leg gave out, and the Texan dropped to the floor. Groaning, the Texan stared cross-eyed into the barrel of the revolver nearly touching his nose.

"You like to bully people, mister?" Martin asked.

The Texan looked from the gun barrel up to Martin's face and his skin turned white as his bravado fled.

"From the way you act, I bet you do. Maybe I ought to teach you a lesson about that."

"Bucho!"

The Texan's eyes widened. "Not now, boss," he called.

"Yes, now."

Martin stepped back and risked a glance at the man standing in the doorway. He was slender and clean-cut, as tall as Martin, with similar angular features. His dark eyes met Martin's with authority, and from the cut of his suit, Martin doubted he was only a foreman.

"What is this?" the man demanded.

"Nothing, Mister Terraza," the bartender said.

Martin looked at the bartender with a deep frown. Then he understood. If the bartender got these three in trouble with their employer, they would charge him a heavy price.

"This gentleman owes me thirty cents," Martin said to Mister Terraza. "For my beer and disturbing my peace."

"He's one of Alvarado's men," the Texan countered loudly. "Bold as brass, he comes in here like it don't mean nothing."

Terraza stared down at the Texan, still on his knees. "We don't own this place, Bucho. He's entitled to a drink here, no matter who employs him. Understand?"

The Texan's mouth hardened.

"Now get out of here. I'll deal with the three of you later."

The Texan rose, cast a last warning glance at Martin, then retreated outside with his companions trailing in his wake. Crooked Nose muttered a curse as he passed, but Martin ignored it and watched them disappear beyond the swinging doors before letting down the hammer on the revolver. He reversed it and extended it to the man in the fine suit.

"This belongs to the Mexican. I only meant to borrow it."

The man took the gun and smiled.

"Three against one is not fair odds. Even one against Bucho is bad, especially for one so light."

Martin shrugged. "I do what I have to."

The man tucked the revolver under his arm and reached into his pocket.

"Please accept my apology, and another drink on me." He laid coins on the counter. Martin considered them, then shook his head.

"I appreciate the gesture, sir, but it's neither your apology nor your money I need."

"Ah." The man nodded. "An honorable settlement is what you desire."

Martin's jaw tightened. He'd spoken wrong. Now he kept his mouth shut rather than make himself more of a fool.

At his silence, the man only offered his hand. "I am Fernando Lopez Terraza."

Martin remembered Lolita's warning and hesitated, but this man offered his hand in friendship, and he grasped it. "Martin. I've heard about your family."

"Obviously nothing good if you're working for Luis Alvarado."

"Not exactly, only rumors."

Fernando studied him for a moment. "May I buy you a drink? No bribe, no pretense. I'm curious to know where you come from, Mister Martin."

"Just Martin. It's easier for people to remember."

"And quicker to say when you're in trouble." Fernando smiled at his own joke. "I had a sister who used to say that."

Martin's skin tingled at the distant memory of his mother saying those words. "It's a good saying."

"Well, about that drink?"

"Thank you, but I better be on my way."

Fernando nodded. "Good day to you."

"And to you." Martin left, checking the street before he stepped out. He was aware of Fernando Terraza watching him from the door as he crossed the street and walked back to the wagon.

Lolita stood on the boardwalk, arms crossed, tapping her foot.

"So, you got a drink, I see."

"Only half."

"Did that man have anything to do with you having only half?"

He followed her nod to Terraza standing outside the saloon, the gun belts draped over his shoulder. Martin shook his head.

"No." He gripped a crate and loaded it into the wagon.

"Stay away from him," Lolita hissed in his ear. "Do you know who that man is?"

"I know his name and that he saved me from killing a man. Besides that, what's some old feud got to do with me?" She recoiled from his question, but he felt no shame. "You can never tell what a person is like until you get to know them, señorita."

She stared at him, mouth softened, while he loaded the supplies. "I'll not say a word about it, but if word reaches Señor Luis, you better run."

"Thanks for the warning." He helped her onto the seat and climbed up beside her. They drove back to the hacienda in silence.

Answers

Winter passed and yielded to the warm days of spring. Martin passed the time working odd tasks around the hacienda in addition to his stable work. He wanted to learn how to ride and train the horses, but that required working with the wranglers, including Kell, and that thought sickened him.

One day, after turning a handful of special saddle and coach horses into the back pasture, he watched as Kell climbed onto the back of a speckled red horse. They had blindfolded the mare and pinned her against the tall breaking pen fence. Kell gripped the hackamore and settled heavily into the saddle, his big spurs poised to rake the spotted flanks.

"Let 'er go, boys!"

The men jumped back, pulling the blindfold. The horse shrieked and leaped into a hard tirade. Kell raked her flanks with those spurs, drawing blood. The mare screamed in pain and kicked her hind legs against the snubbing post.

Martin watched and felt his heart sink.

True to her mustang heritage, the mare had spirit, enough to give her a proud look in her eye and a strong stride, but as time passed with Kell in the saddle cutting her flanks and hauling back against her mouth, she tired. Martin heard about this horse from the men around the table in the evenings, how she kept fighting, and Kell, ever confident, bragged about how he was going to break her. Over the last few days, they deprived her of food and water and kept her standing with front and hind legs hobbled, yet she fought on, and while the men cheered Kell, Martin silently cheered the horse. Not long into this fight, however, Martin sensed it was near the end.

He did not know how long it went on, but weak and exhausted, the mare slowed her bucking.

Kell whooped in triumph. Then the mare bolted and ran headlong into the fence, turning her body at the last moment, throwing her weight into it, causing the posts and planks to pop with the strain. Kell, unseated by the force, tilted sideways, and as the mare jerked back to the left, he dropped to the hard ground. She kicked at him, and Kell scrambled under the rails to safety. Finding the object of her torture out of reach, the mare limped away following the fence.

Reaching through the slats, Martin tried to offer her some grain from the small stash he kept in his pocket and nearly lost his hand when she snapped her teeth at him.

"Leave her be, gray boy!"

Martin met Kell's red faced glare. He was no longer startled by the man, but anger, primed by fear, still struck through him.

Kell marched around the breaking pen toward him. Martin straightened teeth and fists clenched, ready to fight. Kell stood before him for a moment, fists balled, ready. Then the hardness in his face eased, and he glanced at the horse. Reaching out, he gripped a rail and scaled the fence. The mare shied away, but Kell caught the long hackamore and brought her up short. He jerked the mare toward the center of the pen. The mare, her spirit still in the fight, barred her teeth and charged Kell, nipping him in the forearm. Martin nodded once in approval.

Cursing the horse, Kell drew his knife and plunged it into the speckled neck.

The mare reared nearly knocking Kell in the head, yanking free of the blade and sending a spray of blood spattering into the dust. Now, any fight she might have given was destined to fail but she charged Kell and drove him from the pen a second time.

Martin's hands curled into white-knuckled fists as he watched the horse stumble around the corral. A sense of helplessness mixed with rage at the useless waste.

The mare, blood pouring down her neck staggered away from the fence, turned once as though looking for a way to escape. Then, raising her head to the sky, she bellowed a mournful whinny as her legs gave out. Her proud body wilted as her spirit faded, set free on her final breath, her cry carrying and echoing off the buildings. All around the ranch, the other horses responded in a chaotic chorus that sounded angry, sorrowful, and afraid.

Throat tight, stomach turning, and chest burning, Martin glared openly at Kell who gazed in apparent satisfaction at the dead horse.

"You deserved that," he growled and spat tobacco juice through the slats into the horse's glazed eye. "Good for nothin' bitch."

Martin's legs and arms quivered with rage. Kell gave him a single glance, sneering before he turned his back.

The pent-up rage broke loose. Martin leaped onto Kell's broad shoulders sending both into the dirt. He gained his feet first and kicked Kell across the face snapping his head back. It thumped hollowly against the hard-packed earth. He kept kicking, sending Kell's teeth flying. He stomped Kell's hand, then buried his boot toe in the man's midsection before something struck him from behind and pinned him against the breaking coral fence.

"You gone loco?" a short Mexican called Chico shrieked.

"Settle down you wildcat!" another voice ordered. "It's just an old scrub pony."

"He had no right!" Martin screamed struggling to shake loose, but four men put their weight against him, rendering his struggle useless, but he was too mad for this fact to register. All he wanted was to kill Kell.

Armand knelt beside Kell as the big man sat up slowly and rolled to his feet. He tested his jaw and spat in the dust running his tongue over the stubs of his rotten teeth. Then, he leveled a glare at Martin and took a step toward him. Armand stopped him.

"Don't!"

Kell glared at the foreman. "He ain't got no right to jump me like that."

"I wish he'd jumped you sooner." Armand closed the distance between them, and though he was a head shorter than the Texan, his carriage conveyed all the force of a hurricane about to make landfall. "You've killed three of this herd already with the way you ride. You had no right to kill another like that."

Running a hand over his mouth, Kell spat again. "Alvarado doesn't keep me for my way with horses," he said. "He keeps me around for killing."

Armand's jaw hardened. He looked between the two men as their glares locked on each other. Kell looked away first.

"Saddle up," Armand ordered him. "You'll ride to the south border and haze strays."

Kell blinked. "That's two days ride one way."

Armand grinned mockingly. "So, you'll have plenty of time to think about how you'll repay Señor Alvarado for another horse."

Growling in anger, Kell swept up his hat and marched away toward the barn. Armand watched him go then turned to Martin.

"Let him loose," he ordered.

Chico chuckled as he stepped back. "You're one crazy son-of-a-bitch!"

Martin shook his arms. Already he could feel bruises forming where they gripped his arms. His gaze held Armand's. The foreman shook his head.

"Don't keep angering him," Armand warned. "He will kill you one day."

Martin glanced down at his bloodied knuckles, and then back up at Armand. "I don't care much for men like him."

"Neither do I," Armand said. "But Señor Alvarado hired him for a purpose as he said."

Martin clenched his teeth and turned to the trough outside the pen to wash the blood from his hands.

"Señor Alvarado wishes for you to join him for supper tonight," Armand added.

Martin frowned in puzzlement. "What for?"

Armand shook his head as he gripped the buckle of his cartridge belt with his left hand. His right rested on the coiled whip he carried.

"I don't know, and I don't suggest you ask." Armand turned away toward the cookhouse, head down in apparent contemplation.

Splashing water over his face and head, Martin looked at the main house and wondered. Suddenly, Kell burst from the barn, astride his horse at a full run. He turned the big animal straight for Martin.

With an instant to react, Martin leaped over the tough and dove for cover, expecting Kell to renew the fight, but the big man rode on up the rise, laughing and whooping as he went.

Straightening, Martin rose and dusted himself off, caking his wet hands with mud. He watched Kell ride hard into the distance until the rattle of a carriage drew his attention to the far end of the yard. It was a fine black coach pulled by a pair of proud Andalusian horses, a rig for a person of means. It rolled to the front of the house where the driver drew rein and climbed down from the high seat.

Señor Alvarado himself descended the front steps and offered his hand as the driver opened the door. A woman dressed in a dark green traveling gown stepped out and the two spoke briefly before Alvarado led her inside, leaving Lolita to handle the baggage.

Deciding the rest of his work could wait, Martin hurried to help her.

"What are you doing?" she demanded as he lifted a trunk onto his back and silently hoped he would not regret it later.

"The horses can wait a few minutes, ma'am, if you'll just hand me one of those valises." Before she could protest, he took the bigger of the two from her.

She gaped at him, then hissed. "This is not your concern. Armand will kill you."

"If you are his woman, as he claims, he would do this himself." He gestured toward the door. "If we hurry, he'll never know."

With a growl of banked fury, she gathered what she could of the luggage and led him inside.

From the parlor, he heard Alvarado and the woman speaking in hushed tones as he passed. No intelligible words reached him.

Lolita led him to one of the many extra rooms at the front of the house.

"Put it in the corner there." She nodded toward the window beside the bureau.

Martin set the case on the bed and lowered the trunk to the floor.

"No, not like that." Lolita skirted the bed and gripped the trunk handle. Her hand touched his, and she stopped. Her usually blazing spirit ebbed into gentle warmth. She gazed up at him.

"Thank you," she said.

It was a new thing from her. In the months since coming here, she had insulted and berated him, but never once did he feel she spoke with genuine anger. Now he knew for sure.

She drew a deep breath and held it as her lower lip curled back between her teeth in uncertainty, also a new expression. She looked down, blushing.

Knowing the effort it took her to express gratitude, Martin's heart warmed. He cupped her chin and gently guided her eyes back to his.

"You're welcome," he said sincerely, hoping she would understand how much he meant it. He knew what it would cost both of them if he showed how he truly felt at that moment. Drawing back, he flashed a smile and left her alone in the room, staring down at her hands.

At the front door, he met Chico, burdened with the second trunk. The little Mexican grinned at him.

"Next time you tangle with Kell," he said softly, "warn me so I can sell tickets, eh?"

Martin smiled grimly. "Alright, Chico, *if* it happens again."

"*Bueno*. I can make a lot of money off that."

Martin shook his head as the Mexican stepped past him, headed for the guest room. He glanced toward the sitting room, where Alvarado and the lady visitor still spoke. Alvarado glanced up, and their eyes met briefly, but Martin could read nothing in the old face, though a chill seeped into his blood. With a wave of his hand, Alvarado returned his attention to his guest with a deceptively warm smile.

Martin stepped outside and pulled the door shut. He wondered if the guest had anything to do with his invitation to attend supper in the main house. Soon enough, he would know, but in the time he worked here, he learned there was a side to Alvarado that worried Martin.

The coach rolled away toward the barn, breaking Martin's train of thought. He followed it and helped the driver unhitch the team.

Despite being used to the confines of the bunkhouse, the spacious dining hall with its dark walls smothered Martin, as though an unseen entity wrapped its arms around him and squeezed. Alvarado sat at the head of the long table when Martin followed Lolita in. At his right sat the woman who arrived that afternoon. Years of wisdom showed in her pale face, made more so in contrast with the black veil she wore. From her neck hung a sparkling array of diamonds framed against her skin by the low-slung collar of her dark blue gown. She glanced up at him with the air of a queen measuring something of interest to her.

Alvarado stood and extended his hand in a formal introduction.

"Martin, I wish to introduce Señorita Eva Maria Garcia de San Marco."

The woman offered her hand. From the recesses of his mind, the lessons his mother taught him returned. He took her hand and bowed over it.

"Señorita."

She smiled, pleased. She turned to Alvarado and, in Spanish, expressed her surprise that he had manners.

Alvarado dismissed it as something Martin had probably learned in a book. Then he gestured to the chair to his left. "Sit."

Martin obeyed and placed the napkin on his lap. He felt awkward in his effort to not seem out of place, but the woman's attention made him blush.

"I apologize if my manners are poor," Martin said. "My lessons were long ago."

"Don't apologize," Eva said. "I'm really quite impressed and curious to know how you learned."

"My mother was very adamant that I learn proper etiquette. She taught me herself."

"Oh? Who was your mother?"

"Maitea."

The woman frowned and sat back as Lolita served her. "I'm not familiar with that name. Where does she live?"

"She's dead, ma'am," Martin said, hiding the pang of loss he felt. After all the years that had passed, he still missed her. "We lived in Baton Rouge."

The woman nodded. "I've heard of the place, but I've always departed from Port Arthur when leaving for Spain."

"Yes, ma'am." Martin offered Lolita a sheepish thank you as she served him, but her face was unreadable, and further unnerved him.

"Tell us about your mother," Alvarado ordered. "You told me she once lived here. How is it she left this country?"

Martin shrugged. "She only ever told me she had differences with my grandmother. I was too young to remember much."

"And your father?" Eva pressed. "What of him?"

"He was an American. He worked at the ranch where my mother grew up. They fell in love and were married. A year after I was born, he went north, and the Kiowa killed him."

"A shame." Eva picked up her wineglass and seemed to think for a moment. "What did your mother look like?"

Martin reached into his pocket for the daguerreotype he had carried every day since his mother's death. It was small and housed in a protective brass case, which he opened before extending it to the woman.

"This is my father and mother on their wedding day."

She took the portrait in her long fingers and blinked at the image, then leaned over and shared it with Alvarado. Martin searched their expressions as they conferred in whispered Spanish. Alvarado's face was unreadable; the woman was excited.

Closing the case with a solid *snap,* the woman returned it to him with a smile. "I may know where to find your family."

Martin blinked in surprise and glanced at Alvarado. "Are you sure?"

The woman nodded and cast a knowing smile at Alvarado.

Suddenly excited, Martin fought back the urge to press the woman for more information. A sense that she was holding back something nagged him. He asked the first question without rushing his words.

"Where do you think my family is?"

She set down her spoon and folded her hands, studying him for a long moment.

"How old are you, Martin?"

Her question confused him. "Twenty, I think. I was born in the fall."

"And you said your mother's name was Maitea. Did she have other names?"

Martin fought to remember the name. His mother had spoken it only twice, and the memory returned to him with painful effort.

"Maitea Carmelita Helena Mercer." The name came haltingly from his American tongue, the pronunciation clear and correct because it had been the way his mother said it.

"Was it?"

Martin nodded. Alvarado frowned, and the back of his neck prickled as Martin studied him. The old man was fishing for something, what he was unsure.

"Mister Alvarado..."

"*Señor* Alvarado, if you please."

Martin nodded, accepting the correction.

"Sir, I'm not asking anything except for answers. I just want to know what happened to my family."

Alvarado frowned as his fingers tapped the table beside his untouched bowl of soup. Silence lingered long over the table before the old man spoke again.

"It's an old Spanish custom for children to carry the names of both parents, and sometimes even the grandparents. It's a way of tracing our lineage." He paused and watched Martin's reaction. "Your mother would have kept her maiden name and added your father's to it. Since Mercer is a gringo name, I assume she left out her maiden name." He leaned forward, his expression friendly for the first time. "Or she never had one. There is more I will tell you later," he whispered as he patted Martin's wrist and took up his spoon for the first time.

Martin's appetite was gone, and for this, he received many threatening stares from Lolita. No matter how hard he tried, though, he could not make himself eat.

He was thankful when Eva excused herself. Alvarado stood and took her hand.

Eva apologized for retiring early and expressed her desire to leave for home early in the morning.

Alvarado kissed her hand and thanked her for her company. Eva glanced back at Martin and smiled.

"I hope you find your family, Martin," she said. "I feel strongly that you will."

"Thank you, señorita." He bowed as she sank into a curtsy that remained graceful despite her age. How she remained unmarried puzzled him.

Alvarado turned to the hall and gestured for him to follow with a firm but kind command. "Come."

Martin followed him through a side door into the parlor where the two of them sat the night Martin came to the hacienda.

"Do you enjoy tobacco?" Alvarado asked, opening a dark wooden box on the sideboard and surveying the contents.

"I tried a pipe once, but I don't reckon it was tobacco."

"Oh, how did you know?" He selected a cigar, smelling it before clipping the end.

"It smelled sweeter than tobacco." Martin stood near the door, feeling hunger creep back to him. He surveyed the room, and his attention came to rest on a painting above the mantel.

"Me in my youth," Alvarado said, noticing Martin's interest. "Long ago."

The image was unmistakable, but in youth, Alvarado bore a vague resemblance to Fernando Terraza. The features and build were much the same, though Alvarado was longer of limb.

Martin stared as his mind struggled to fully comprehend what his eyes were seeing, and his ears hearing and reconciling the two.

Alvarado filled two glasses of wine and brought one to Martin.

"I didn't want to speak of it in the señorita's presence, but as a man, I think you'll understand."

Martin took the glass and met Alvarado's gaze with a silent question.

Alvarado smiled and paced toward the row of windows held in iron frames.

"I'm sure you understand a man's need for a woman," Alvarado said slowly.

The memory of brightly painted women enticing men to the upper floors of the rooming house where he and his mother had lived remained vivid because of the mystery it held in his childhood. During the war, he learned of prostitution and came to dislike it in principle. Though he felt the need, he craved companionship more. "Yes, I believe I do," he responded.

"And, you also have heard the story about my courtship with Carmelita de La Rosa y Lopez?"

"Yes."

Alvarado scoffed and sipped from his glass. "Well, she was the only woman I ever really loved. After her, all others simply satisfied my animal needs. I had no desire to take a wife." He shrugged and turned away from the windows, pacing. "I've had many women in my bed through the years and have fathered several children, including, I suspect, your mother."

Martin met his gaze, unsure if he liked the story. He never knew what he would find when he came here. If this was the truth, he had no choice but to accept it.

"You, yourself, can see the resemblance," Alvarado said, gesturing to his portrait as he paced past the dead fireplace.

Martin glanced up at the portrait again but saw the resemblance as a bare suggestion.

Alvarado sank into a chair beside the hearth, the same one he sat on the night Martin had come in from the rain.

"I'm growing old," he said with a sigh. "Someday, I will leave this world, and I wish this land to go to someone. I would prefer it to be one who shares my heritage."

"What of the others?" Martin asked. When Alvarado silently questioned him, he continued. "You said you fathered many children. Certainly, there are some whose heritage you're more certain of than mine. You said yourself; you only suspect I'm your grandson."

A dish clattered loudly in the dining room. Martin glanced toward the open door and briefly met Lolita's glare as she turned and hurried into the kitchen.

Alvarado chuckled. "Many of them I doubt I'm their father. Others already have an inheritance from the fathers who raised them, but you!" He sprang from his chair with impressive agility and stood within inches of Martin. "You have no one!"

Martin searched the man's face. Something seemed strange. Perhaps it was the light, or perhaps it was because he had searched for so long, never expecting to learn the truth that knowing felt strange. He looked down, trying to make sense of it all.

"Of course," Alvarado went on with a dismissive wave of his hand. "I'm not promising you anything. If you stay here, work hard, and prove you can carry the Alvarado name with pride, you will stand to inherit one of the biggest *ranchos* in Texas."

Staring into the fireplace's charred walls, Martin thought about this. As much as he knew the proposal would entice most, the prospect of owning a ranch like this held little appeal to him. What he wanted more was to know who he was and know his family's story. He looked into Alvarado's eyes and ached to believe this man.

"If what you say is true, I hope I won't disappoint you."

Alvarado smiled broadly and patted Martin's shoulder. "I doubt you will." Apparently satisfied that the matter was closed, he turned back to his chair, his back no longer as bent as before.

Martin swallowed his wine in a single toss of his glass.

"If you'll excuse me, señor, I have chores I must finish."

Alvarado frowned at him. "Would you rather not leave them to someone else?"

Martin shook his head. "It's my responsibility."

With a shrug of his features, Alvarado dismissed him with a wave of his hand. Martin thanked him and left through the kitchen door. Lolita did not look up from her work when he passed, and he did not wait for her to acknowledge him. His thoughts were too scattered to deal with her windblown moods.

He went to the barn, and halfway through filling a bucket with grain, his hands slowed as what Alvarado had said settled into his understanding. Still, he struggled to believe his mother was illegitimate, raised by *peons*. How could she have been so refined after being raised by servants?

But she also had raised her son in a brothel, making fine dresses for the parlor girls, who plied their trade in the brightly painted rooms below their attic home. Would a well-bred lady reduce herself to such a state over an argument with her mother?

Martin shook his head. His mother had no other choice, and a seamstress was the best she could do. He could accept being a bastard for himself, but he refused to think of his mother as such.

He shoved the scoop deep into the grain. By the time he filled the bucket, his thoughts remained a gentle roar inside his skull, but nothing seemed clearer in his mind.

Wildcat

The border ran north and south along the wash, where the last trickle of spring runoff cut a narrow swath through the sand. Martin drew rein at the edge and stared across onto Terraza land. He saw no cattle, but Chico nodded toward the rock outcropping less than a mile across the wash.

"Bet you ten dollars; there are cattle in those rocks."

"Do we dare go over there?" Martin asked, uneasy at the idea of trespassing on Terraza range.

"Who's going to know? There ain't a Terraza rider in miles." He kicked his little pinto down the slope. "Come on. You can always run back here if you get scared."

Martin bit his lip. He disliked the idea, but returning to the roundup empty handed guaranteed mockery. It had been at Alvarado's insistence that he took part in this operation, miles away from anywhere at the mercy of Kell and the others. Though their treatment had improved since Alvarado announced Martin would be his heir, a subtle threat remained in Kell's every look. If it had not been for Chico, Martin would not have slept the last week.

With a kick to his mount's flanks, he followed, hoping the Mexican was right. Continuously scanning the open country around them, they approached the rocks and found the outcrop a mile wide and two miles long.

"This isn't going to be a quick task, Chico."

"Ah, so what?" Chico turned his horse up a narrow trail. "Terrazas never come this far south."

"Then what are those fresh tracks from? A ghost?"

Chico turned in the saddle and looked to where Martin pointed.

"Ah, those are mine," he responded with a grin. He kicked his horse again. "Come on. I don't want to spend more time here than I have to."

Martin knew little about cattle, but he knew tracks, and the fresh, shod hoof prints did not belong to Chico's mustang. He glanced back toward the wash. He could leave Chico on his own, but if trouble came, he doubted he could live with having left Chico to harm. Martin heeled his bay horse forward, but the animal balked at the idea, and Martin had to kick the gelding hard to get him up the slope.

They reached the top and looked out on the green late spring land.

"See." Chico grinned. "I told you we'd find cattle up here."

"Yeah, and they're not ours."

Down below, a herd of twenty head milled in a small canyon flanked by two riders on horses Martin did not recognize.

Chico watched, and his tanned face lost a little color. Then he smiled.

"They won't be there long. A lion stalks them."

Martin watched a long, lanky form move down along the canyon wall. From their position in the canyon, neither man saw the cat, nor would their horses alert to its presence with it approaching from downwind. He turned the bay along the canyon edge, searching for a way down.

"Loco!" Chico's voice was shrill, as he realized what Martin was doing. Martin ignored him.

He found a chimney, rocky and sloped gently enough he could descend on foot, but too steep for the bay. He pulled his rifle from the scabbard and started down.

The herd and riders were out of sight beyond the chimney's edge. Martin scrambled down, half sliding as he went. Then he heard a growl and the screams of horse and man. Shots broke out, and as Martin came into view, he saw the second rider charge the cat as it stood over the first man. The cat leaped, knocking the second rider from his horse three hundred yards away.

Martin knew he could not cover the distance in time. He dropped beside a rock and levered a round into the rifle's chamber. He sighed and held his breath as the rider tried to rise. When he fired, the cat staggered and looked up. Martin worked the leaver and fired a second round into the cat's face. The cat dropped, falling beside the rider, kicking in the throes of death.

Moving cautiously, Martin approached the cat as it grew still. Though blood still pulsed from the wound in the animal's side, every muscle relaxed as the life drained away from the cougar.

Martin recognized the man lying beside the cat as the Mexican from the saloon. He was dead, slashed through the jugular. A strange sadness passed over Martin and was gone as he moved to the other man, who still breathed. Martin kneeled beside him, shading his face from the sun. His dark eyes opened, and Martin saw fear and pain in them.

Behind him, Chico let out a string of curses in Spanish as he dropped the reins of Martin's bay and dismounted.

"You know who he is, gray boy?" Chico asked in English. "That's Filipe Terraza. Fernando Terraza's son. Grandson of Santiago Terraza. You bring him back to Terraza *rancho*, and you'll not ride away."

"I'm not leaving him here." Martin shrugged his vest and unbuttoned his shirt.

"Mister, he isn't wrong," Filipe said weakly.

Martin's heart sank. He did not know if the Terrazas knew him as Alvarado's grandson, but even as one of Alvarado's hired hands, the Terrazas likely wanted him dead for trespassing on their land. He knew for certain if he took Filipe to Alvarado's ranch, Alvarado would kill him or leave him to die slowly for lack of care. Martin had no choice.

"You got a mama?" Martin asked as he tore his shirt into bandages.

"Yes."

"Think of her and how she'd feel not knowing what happened to you. Women can be funny about things like that. Especially mothers." He cut the sleeve away from Filipe's left arm, which had taken the worst of the cat's attack, and wrapped most of the makeshift bandage around the wounded limb.

"Let's go. We'll only complicate things by staying here." Chico grabbed his arm. Martin jerked free and glared up at his companion.

"Go on back if you're so inclined. I'm not leaving him to die."

Chico blinked, and Martin went back to bandaging the wounds.

"You can't take him to Alvarado. They'll kill him, and the town is too far."

"I'll take him to the Terraza ranch. What they do with me is my concern."

Chico looked grim. "If they don't kill you for being an Alvarado, Señor Luis will have you whipped when you come back to the rancho. He certainly will disown you as his kin."

Jaw flexing, Martin realized he was burning a bridge. But a closed door meant less than a man's life, even if the man was the son of someone who would kill him for no other reason than the fate of his birth. Martin went on, committing his mind to knowing he would never fully belong.

"Go on, Chico," he said, staring into the eyes of Filipe Terraza, confident he was doing the right thing.

Chico sighed heavily. "I hope you know what you're doing, amigo. *Adios*." He climbed onto his paint and galloped back toward the wash and Alvarado land.

"I thank you, stranger," Filipe said a moment later through tight lips.

"Don't thank me yet," Martin said, leaving him to bring the bay close to offer shade while he rounded up the other horses. "It's still a long ride ahead." He gave Filipe no chance to reply. He caught the horses, then loaded the dead man on one, and brought the palomino for Filipe, who now sat up braced against his good arm.

"I'll be able to ride alone," he said.

"Are you sure?" Martin brought him a canteen. Filipe nodded.

"If I fall off, you can tie me on." He took a swallow and handed back the canteen with a weak smile.

"Right now, you falling off is the least of my worries." Martin took his arm and pulled him to his feet. He helped the wounded man into the saddle, then climbed onto his own horse. "You'll have to direct me some. I don't know the way to the Terraza ranch."

Filipe nodded south. "Follow this wash 'til you come to a trail. Then head west along it. It will take you there."

Already, Filipe swayed in the saddle, but Martin hesitated to tie him on his horse. He knew what damage ropes could do and, with the chance his existing wounds would fester, the last thing Filipe needed was further injury. After a mile, Martin took to riding alongside, holding Filipe in the saddle. It was over ten miles to the Terraza ranch. By the time night fell, he gave up and rode double with the wounded man leading his own horse and the horse with its dead burden.

Filipe was out of his head by the time the main gate of Terraza Rancho emerged into view among the shadows. Brightened by the moonlight, it became a beacon on the open, barren land. Martin paused at the end of the trail leading to the door, his eyes tracing the top of the fortress. He expected to see guards pacing the fire step, but nothing moved. A sound, a motion, no matter how slight, would have eased his mind.

Filipe stirred and raised his head, staring at the gates, delirious. Martin felt him tense and groan softly.

"*Lo siento*," he whispered.

Filipe shook his head. "You've already done more than..." He tensed as another wave of pain passed over him.

"Easy, now." Martin shifted his grip on the reins. "I'll take you up there."

He nudged the horse forward at the same slow walk that had carried them over many miles. All the while, he watched, waited, knowing the strong likelihood of a bullet ending his life.

They stopped less than ten feet from the heavy, iron banded doors built to hold off attacks by Comanches.

"Hello!" Martin called. Silence answered.

"Why don't the guards answer?" Filipe asked.

"I doubt they're sleeping." Martin listened a moment longer and then called again in Spanish for Fernando. This time, the response was a pair of rifles extending from above the gate. Martin released the reins, raised his left hand, and called out in Spanish to see Fernando.

"He sleeps, *gringo*," one snarled. "Be on your way."

"I have his son, Filipe, here. He needs care, and I won't leave him on the doorstep."

The speaker scoffed. "Señor Filipe is in the hills, far from here."

"A cougar attacked him. I've brought him here for help." Despite the rise of anger, Martin kept his tone calm. His words affected a sober silence from the man.

"Be on your way," the voice said again, and when Martin remained, someone fired a shot into the dirt between the horse's legs. The palomino jumped and bucked. Martin gripped the horn and held on to keep them both in the saddle, but Filipe, weak and disoriented by pain, went limp. When he fell, Martin did his best to ease the fall, but they hit hard, and he felt the shock in his left shoulder as the joint popped out of socket. Fortunately, the horse turned and bolted down the trail with the others in tow, sparing Martin and Filipe from being trampled.

"The next will find your heart, *gringo*."

Martin ignored the guard and turned to Filipe. His wounds bled again, and Martin did what he could to stop it.

"Didn't you hear me, *gringo*!"

"Paco." Filipe's voice was weak. Martin doubted it carried to the guard, but the young man had spirit. He filled his lungs and called out again. "Paco!"

In the faint moonlight, Martin saw the guard's mouth soften.

"Señor Filipe?"

With great effort, Filipe raised his head so the man could see his face.

"Let us in."

The guard hesitated, but he and the other guard lowered their weapons. Beyond the wall, voices shouted, and the gate opened. Martin felt relief at the sight of Fernando, shirt untucked, coming toward them with a lantern.

"Your father's coming, Filipe."

Filipe's eyes closed. As the lantern light fell across them, Martin looked up, and Fernando stopped dead in his tracks.

"What is this Alvarado scum doing on my land?" he said a moment later.

"I mean no harm," Martin said. He rose and faced Fernando, raising his right hand. "I freely admit to trespassing, but a cougar attacked your son and his companion. The other was killed, and I brought Filipe here to be cared for."

Fernando frowned. He gave orders in Spanish, and two men carried Filipe inside.

"What do you hope to gain by this?"

Martin shook his head. "Nothing. Only, I understand a mother's grief and how not knowing what happened to her child can make that grief worse."

Fernando's expression softened. "Where's the other man?"

"Down the road on one of the horses I led in."

"Paco!"

The guard stepped forward, and Fernando ordered him to track down the horses, since it was his shot that spooked them. Paco grudgingly obeyed and disappeared into the night.

"Ordinarily, I would turn you away," Fernando said. "Considering the circumstances, I will give you what I can, but cannot let you inside the gate."

Martin nodded that he understood.

Fernando looked him over. "Come to the gate. I'll have someone look at that shoulder."

He could not refuse what Fernando Terraza offered. His arm hung useless, and the pain nearly took his breath away.

"Bucho!"

He nearly groaned when he looked up into the face of the big Texan from town. He held up his good hand.

"No trouble."

Though Bucho's face was grim, he put down his rifle against the wall.

"He can fix your shoulder," Fernando explained, casting a warning look at the Texan.

Reluctantly, Martin let the Texan guide him over to a hitching post outside the gate.

"Lean over it with the rail across your chest," he said.

Martin glanced at Fernando whose unsympathetic expression offered no invitation for trust. Deciding, he had nothing left to lose, Martin followed Bucho's instructions. Then Bucho sat on the ground beneath the rail and took Martin's arm.

"Don't let me pull you over," Bucho said.

Martin nodded as Bucho took his wrist. With the other hand, he gripped Martin's upper arm. Then Bucho pulled with the full weight of his body.

Martin felt as though his arm might tear off his body, but the muscles gave up quickly as Bucho overpowered them and guided the joint back into place. The pain eased, and as Bucho relaxed his grip, the numbness left Martin's fingers. Still, his shoulder throbbed.

"You'll want to put that in a sling for a few days," Bucho said.

Martin nodded; his throat too tight to speak.

Without a word, Bucho took up his rifle and stood beside the gate. Not even Fernando spoke as they waited. Once Paco returned with the horses, Martin climbed onto his bay.

"Don't let the sunrise find you on this land," Fernando commanded. "I give you your life for saving my son, but no more."

Martin bowed his head respectfully and turned the bay down the road, heading east. With no bedroll and no provisions for the trail, he had little choice but to find his way back to the Alvarado camp and try to get his gear. He was uncertain what to expect. The very least his grandfather could do under the circumstances was let him have what he bought himself. Less than an hour of night remained when he rode into the camp. The cook, already at work, went to Armand's bed and woke him before Martin dismounted. Within moments, the camp came alive in silent motion. Martin went quickly to the gear wagon and collected his bedroll and rifle. Then he turned and found ten men fanning out, surrounding him and cornering him against the wagon.

"Where are you going?" Armand asked.

"Leaving."

Armand chuckled. "So you're just going to tuck tail and run?" A chorus of chuckles, sneers, and overall agreement ran through the men.

Martin glanced around at them, sizing them up. They had waited a long time for this moment, and a few of them grinned in anticipation. Kell grinned the widest, his mouth a mottled dark patch on his ugly face.

"I want no part of this," he told Armand. "If I can't help a man in need, I want nothing to do with this place."

The lines of Armand's face deepened in the shadows from the chuck wagon's lantern. He stepped forward into shadow, and his face disappeared, but what Martin had seen was already enough.

"You're not worthy of the Alvarado name. You betrayed us and helped our enemy." Armand stood close, rubbing his knuckles. He seethed theatrically. "You don't walk away from that."

Martin knew it was coming, but was slow to react. Armand's left caught him in the middle of his stomach, just below the ribs, and forced the wind from his lungs. Doubling over, he didn't see the next blow that caught him on the left side and knocked him to the ground. They never let him rise as far as his knees before someone knocked him down again. A boot caught him on the side of the head, stunning him. After that, all he knew was pain and darkness. Armand's voice, growling a command in Spanish, penetrated the men's cheers.

They stripped him of his boots, belt, and vest. When Kell reached into his hip pocket for the watch, he struck out and landed a solid blow on Kell's mouth. Kell reacted by gripping his throat and squeezing. Martin reached up, trying to dig his fingers into Kell's eyes, but Kell held his face out of reach. Darkness descended, consumed Martin, and he felt nothing.

When he stopped fighting, Kell took the watch, pocketed it, then dragged Martin to his horse and threw him across the saddle.

Chico saddled his paint and waited for Kell to saddle his horse. Then they led the bay out through the scrub in the morning twilight. They rode the three miles to the ranch border. There, they brought the bay alongside a gully and shoved Martin's limp body into it. Then Kell, thorough at his job, drew his pistol and cocked it.

"He's good as dead already," Chico protested. "Why waste the bullet?"

"Because he's worth making sure." He fired a round into Martin's back. Mercifully, Martin had lost his senses and did not move. "See. Didn't feel that, *if* he's still breathing." He holstered the revolver and leaned down to gather the bay's reins. "Let's go. I got me an appetite."

Chico lingered beside the gully, staring down at Martin's remains. If he felt remorse, he only showed it with a brief prayer, covering his heart with his hat. He signed himself and kissed his fingers before turning the paint to follow Kell.

The sun rose, bringing with it the heat that drew lizards from hiding. They scurried over rocks and Martin's body with equal caution, wary of the shadows that played over them. Vultures circled, landed, and moved close, but when he moved, they fell back and waited. Martin, with one good arm and no strength, crawled down the gully to an overhang. He knew nothing of what he did, only that he had to flee the vultures and the sun, but as he neared an overhang, he knocked the dirt loose, and the overhang collapsed, burying him. Through the cloud of dust, he stared at the pile of dirt and felt despair descend in a constricting air as oppressive as the building heat of the day. In a mind not quite clear, and a world bleached by the sun, he broke down inside. He thought of the family he long dreamed of meeting and would never know. How close he came to finding out what happened and why his mother had left this place! It all ended here in a dry wash in the middle of land that killed, surrounded by heartless people. He was alone and had no more strength to fight. So, he put his head down and wept silently. Perhaps if he slept, he would not feel the vultures tear into his flesh.

The plume of dust carried high in the windless air. It caught the eye of a rider nearly a mile away.

Paco frowned at it.

"Hey, Jinx," he called to his companion in the day's search for cattle. "See that?"

Jinx squinted. At his age, the sun's glare hurt his eyes.

"Yeah." He shifted the tobacco in his mouth and spat. "Ain't enough wind to stir a devil."

"Maybe we should go see. Could be one of our cows."

Jinx shook his head. "With all the buzzards around, I doubt it's anything we can do much with."

Paco thought for a moment, then shook his head. "We've been all day out here and seen nothing. I'm going to look." He turned his little buckskin and kicked it into a lope.

"You're going to make that ride for nothing!" Jinx hollered after him. He spat again and glanced around at the brush, realizing he'd grown bored with the search. "Awe, hell!" he growled and followed Paco, cussing Mexicans as a whole for the simple fact it made him feel better.

Vultures leaped into the air as Paco drew up short of the wash. He frowned when he saw nothing resembling a steer or cow. Then he moved closer and rode along the edge. Then he saw the form of a man, face down, half his body covered in dirt from a collapsed side of the wash. Paco jumped from his horse and slid down the steep side of the wash. He kneeled beside the body, searching for signs of life.

"What'd you find?"

Paco shook his head. "Must've been *banditos*. They stripped him." Then he turned the man over and recognized the face. He cursed.

"What?"

"The *gringo* from last night, the one who brought Señor Filipe home."

Jinx spat. "Alvarado must not've liked what he did." He worked the plug and settled it between his cheek and lower jaw again. "You're going to have to do most of the digging. My old bones won't take that kind of work."

Paco removed his hat and bowed his head. "Stubborn *pendejo*. I might've liked him." Then Paco saw the exit wound and realized it bled afresh. He reached out and touched the blood to be sure, and then he put his fingers to the parted lips and felt the stir of the man's breath. "He's still alive," he called to Jinx, who had turned away to find a burial site.

"Well, damn it, stop squawking, and do something!" Jinx dismounted and brought his canteen to Paco. "Clean that wound out and get the bleeding stopped."

While Paco worked, he hoped the gringo would wake and show he still had strength, but he remained senseless. Jinx hoped against his better judgement as they wrapped the wounds in his chest and back with Paco's shirt.

"Hopefully, your Mex sweat doesn't infect those wounds."

Paco shot Jinx a look. "Any infection he's going to get, he already has. You see how far he crawled?"

"All the same, ain't nothing out here going to save him. Let's get him on my horse."

Jinx rode double, holding Martin's limp body in the saddle in front of him. When they rode into the yard at Terraza Ranch, Fernando was first to meet them, with his wife, Lucia, close behind.

"What's this?"

"*El gringo*," Paco answered. "The one from last night."

Fernando's lips tightened in anger. "I'll take him."

Jinx handed Martin down to Fernando, who carried him inside.

"The spare room." Lucia cut past him and led the way up the hall past Filipe's room. She turned down the blankets and supported Martin's head as Fernando laid him down. Jaw tight, he unwrapped the improvised bandages.

"It looks bad," Fernando said after examining the wounds. He sighed. "Clean him. Make him comfortable. I'll be back." He marched back outside to where Paco and Jinx watered their horses. "Who did that?"

"Wasn't us, señor," Paco replied. "We would have left him out there."

"Nice to know you have a heart, Paco," Fernando snapped. "Did he say anything? Anything about Alvarado?"

Jinx shook his head. "No. He's been like that since we found him. Never would've known he was still living if he hadn't been bleeding."

Fernando grunted in rage. "Had to be Alvarado. Only he would be so hard."

"Anything we can do to help, señor?" Paco asked, removing his hat. "I feel a little responsible."

Fernando's temper cooled. He shook his head.

"No. You men have done what you could." He nodded in the vague direction of the corral. "Go on about your work."

"Thank you, señor." Paco led his horse away, but Jinx remained behind. He sat on the edge of the water tank and removed his hat.

"Mister Fernando?"

"Yes?"

"I got a real good look at that boy," Jinx said quietly. "Kind of reminds me of someone."

"Who?" Fernando asked over his shoulder.

"Your sister."

Fernando's eyes widened. He turned to face Jinx, who raised his hand, patting the air as though to calm Fernando's fresh rise in temper.

"Just hear me out," he said in that same calm tone. "I ain't saying anything in particular, but something in his face reminds me real strong of her. That's all I'm saying."

Fernando squinted at Jinx.

"You've been out in the sun too long," Fernando said finally.

"Maybe I have." Jinx shook his head. "Truth is you don't know what happened to her and her son. Maybe they died. Maybe they just got lost. Maybe that boy is hers, and he's come back looking for some answers."

Frowning, Fernando turned and stared toward the house. "Go back to your work, Jinx."

"Yes, sir." Jinx pulled on his hat and stood with a sigh. "I will." He led his horse away to the corral, leaving Fernando alone with his thoughts.

Santiago Terraza

Cool stillness surrounded him. In delirium, he believed he had slipped quietly into hell. Now, he wondered if Heaven claimed him by mistake.

He reached for his pocket for the watch, but a strange force held his arm back. In his half-conscious mind, this puzzled him. Earth would have no give. He could move a little, but not enough, and that restriction came from pain and weariness.

His mind cleared, and he could feel soft cloth surrounding his body, like the sheets of the bed where he had lain ill as a child, but that was as far as his mind reached. The sensation faded, and his thoughts grew muddled. He felt as though he floated on the swells of a sea, twisting, bending, and turning on the waves as everything around him grew surreally distant. Then the feeling calmed, and he slowly woke again and heard men's voices speaking in worried tones.

Martin opened his eyes, but the lids were too heavy, and they closed before his vision focused. He tried again to see the men speaking nearby. Their voices were clearer now, speaking Spanish, and his sluggish mind struggled to grasp understanding. He blinked, and the ceiling above cleared. The voices stopped. One man spoke again, and Martin turned his head toward him.

He sat beside the bed, a white-haired man with sharp features and a close-trimmed beard. His eyes sparkled in the lamplight as he smiled a kind smile. His right hand gripped a cane, which he passed to his left and reached out to touch Martin's forehead.

"You live as yet," he said, gently stroking Martin's hair as he tested the warmth of Martin's skin. He turned and spoke again in Spanish to the other man. Martin understood enough to know they talked about him. The other man came near, and Martin recognized Fernando Terraza. Fernando's face creased with worry and darkened with something that remained when the worry lifted.

"Filipe?" Martin asked with an effort. His throat was dry, and he nearly choked as a cough tore through his windpipe. The old man calmly took a glass of water from the bedside table and helped him drink. The coughing left his throat raw and his chest with a sharp pain running through it.

"He will live too," the old man said. "The infection was severe, but he survived. Without you, he would not have lived."

"I don't remember coming back here," Martin said, fighting grogginess. He looked at Fernando. "What happened?"

"Paco and Jinx found you in a wash near the border of our land. You've been beaten and shot. It seems they left you for dead. Jinx said the vultures were about to take their first bite." Fernando's mouth remained tight. Martin knew his presence displeased the man.

"I'm sorry," Martin mumbled.

Fernando waved his hand. "You've nothing to be sorry for. Filipe told me what happened, how the puma jumped him and Alonso, and how you saved him." Martin felt the heat rise in his cheeks. He looked away as Fernando went on. "He also told me there was another man with you who warned you not to go back to the Alvarado herd. It appears you didn't heed his warning."

Martin closed his eyes, searching his memory.

"I needed my gear," he explained when his thoughts finally organized. "Didn't care about my pay, but my gear..." Then he remembered the watch and the picture, and his heart sank into his stomach. He looked from one man to the other. "Did they find anything with me?"

Both men looked grim, and for a moment, Martin feared he had lost the two most valuable things in this world. Then, the old man sat forward, leaning on the cane whose scarred wood matched the gnarled skin of his hands.

"They found only this." The man's expression was gentle as he reached over and picked the daguerreotype off the table and slipped it into Martin's palm. "We had to pry it from your hand to clean the blood away."

Relief washed away the pain. Though the watch too had value, the picture was the only proof he had of his heritage. Without it, he was as lost as any maverick. He closed his eyes and felt thanks in every fiber of his being.

The old man told Fernando he would stay if the younger man had other things to attend. Fernando nodded, calling the old man "abuelo" and telling him not to excite Martin, but even through their Spanish, what Martin understood confused him. His mind was still weak, and he quickly gave up puzzling over their conversation.

"That picture," the old man said, gesturing to Martin's hand. "Is of your mother and father?"

Martin nodded. "Their wedding day."

"Are they dead?"

Again, Martin nodded. "I came here hoping to find what remained of my mother's family. Now..." He shook his head, staring at the brass case. "There's no hope."

The old man nodded. "Alvarado has long hated us. If only he knew the truth, but he would never listen."

"Señor Fernando called you '*grandfather*.' Are you Santiago? The winner of Carmelita's hand?"

The old man chuckled. "Ah, yes. I am Santiago, but a winner..." He shook his head. "That is the story Alvarado never knew, but I like how you put it. It shows openness. If you were truly devoted to Alvarado, you would have called me a thief." He smiled, and Martin felt a sense of familiarity. "Everyone calls me grandfather here, even my son and our hired hands. I'm too old and broken to work anymore. I can only tell stories." He regarded Martin for a moment. "I tell the stories of how our family came to this land from Spain so that my grandchildren will know their heritage. Everyone should know their family's story. Don't you agree?"

As Santiago gazed into his eyes, Martin felt sadness. He looked away, feeling lost and lonely as his throat tightened.

"I think you agree," Santiago said. "That's why you look away. You don't yet know your story, but you will in time, and even if you never know the story of your family, yours will be the beginning of a new line of stories that your children will treasure for generations to come."

As Santiago spoke, the life in his eyes spread, animating his whole lean body. His gnarled hands gestured, artfully emphasizing his words. When he paused, his eyes grew contemplative, and after several moments, he nodded as though deciding something.

"I will share the story with you," he said. "Because of what you did for my grandson, and because…" He shook his head in a subtle theatric gesture. "When you're old, sleeping holds no interest."

Martin smiled at this. He understood and felt honored to have the kind old man's attention.

"I don't know if I can remember it," he said in a quiet apology.

Santiago saw how tired he was. He placed a hand over Martin's.

"It cannot be told all in one night," he said. "What I tell you tonight will only be the beginning."

Martin listened as his eyes grew heavy and finally closed. He felt like a boy again, and in the deep recesses of his memory came the image of his mother telling him a story like this one so long ago time blurred the names and details. He did not know when his mind completely separated from Santiago's lively voice, but he remembered the image of ships tossed in a storm and harboring off the Texas shore.

In the days that followed, Martin regained enough strength to listen without falling asleep, but it was several days longer before he regained enough strength to walk more than the few feet between the bed and the high-backed chair by the window with Santiago's patient help.

Martin was not used to the fussing Filipe's mother and sister bestowed on him. He knew it stemmed from gratitude, and he did his best to accept their care graciously, but he felt smothered. Four days after awaking from fever, Santiago convinced Lucia to let the two young men sit on the veranda outside Martin's room. The day was hot, and this side of the house was in the shade, cool and comfortable.

Filipe sat in a broad, high-backed chair. He smiled when Martin stepped onto the porch with Lucia steadying him and muttering in Spanish about young blood being too eager to heal. She commanded him to sit while she gathered a blanket for him.

"Ma'am, please…"

"A boy as thin as you with much blood to make you'll catch a chill," Lucia countered.

"Calm down, Daughter," Santiago said with an upraised hand, as though to fend off her feisty temper. "Martin has been alone for a long time. I am sure he knows what's best for him."

"He's hardly older than Filipe there," Lucia countered.

"And I'm sure he appreciates your motherly care." Santiago poured wine into small, stemmed glasses. "But he needs room to heal as he must. Like any wild thing, he's not used to so much attention."

Unsure if Santiago meant to flatter him with the comment, Martin watched the red liquid splash into the small glasses and avoided eye contact with Lucia.

Santiago straightened, and without his cane, carefully brought two glasses to Martin and Filipe.

"Don't fret," he told Lucia. "If he becomes chilled, I'll get a blanket for him."

Lucia looked down at Martin, her eyes blazing. He'd faced his share of danger in his life, but women carried their own category of danger against which he had no defense.

She relented by folding the blanket from the bed inside and placing it on the chair beside him. When her cool fingers touched his cheek, it startled him. He looked up into her eyes, now tender with motherly love. She kissed his forehead, then turned to her son and did the same, commanding them to behave. Once she departed, Santiago raised his glass.

"Let us drink," he said. "To consequences."

"Isn't that a little odd, abuelo?" Filipe asked. "It's not as though consequences are ever very good."

"Ah, but that is where your youth puts you at a disadvantage." Santiago raised his glass. "To consequences, whatever they may be."

The old man's toast puzzled Martin, but out of courtesy, he raised his glass and drank.

"I still don't understand," Filipe protested after drinking.

"You will in time." He moved the blanket and sat beside Martin.

"Filipe knows this story well, but he could do to hear it again."

Martin saw Filipe's jaw flex. Santiago saw it too and ignored it.

"Where did I leave off?" Santiago asked rhetorically as he closed his eyes in deep thought.

Thinking for a moment, Martin remembered. "Diego coming ashore was the last I remember."

Santiago smiled, satisfied. "He was my grandfather, a man of light hair and green, gold-flecked eyes, a tall man of lean strength, wise for his youth. He fought for Spanish conquest in the south and earned his land here, whatever land he chose. When he came, he saw the people of this land, Los Indios, living as they had for thousands of years and was fascinated by it. He helped the brothers of San Francisco build their church in the nearby town and taught those that came how to ranch. Their descendants still live on this land today. Maria Luis is the great-granddaughter of the first Indian to bring his family to this rancho. He was given the name Juan by the missionaries. He also brought with him his sister, whom Grandfather Diego fell in love with. It wasn't a quick love, but one that grew with time. When faced with the choice of marrying the daughter of a Spanish don and the Indian maiden, he chose the latter, Helena. She died a year after giving birth to my father. My grandfather married again, this time to the Spanish woman. She bore two sons and a daughter. The daughter went back to Spain, and one son went to California. The two sons of Diego that remained here never got along. They fought over the littlest things. Before Grandfather Diego died, he divided his land equally between them, knowing they would never live together as brothers should."

"That's what became Alvarado land," Filipe offered.

"Yes." Santiago nodded sadly. "The son of the Spanish woman, Manuel, fathered only daughters, the oldest of which married a Spanish man of that name who inherited the land through his wife. The son of the Indian woman, Shiloh, remained here. His sons ran the ranch together, but only I survived to marry."

"How is it, then," Martin asked, "that the rivalry continued? Isn't it usually the father that passes that on?"

Santiago thought for a moment. "Perhaps, but in this case, the daughter of Manuel passed it on to her son. While it seemed quiet in those years, her cunning kept the rivalry going. They bought more land and nearly doubled what they began with. While she was only a woman, she ran that ranch before and after her husband died with all the strength and wisdom of a man. Her son, Luis, has never married."

"He and Abuelo never got along," Filipe added. "Between his arrogance and Abuelo's temper, it's no wonder."

"He doesn't seem to know why," Martin explained, nearly referring to Luis Alvarado as "grandfather," but he caught himself before uttering the first sound. "Señor Alvarado never spoke of his motivations. Only that if we ever met Terraza riders, he didn't care what happened."

Santiago nodded slowly. "Four of our men have been found dead in the last six months. It makes it hard to hire additional help. Those still here have lived and worked here as their fathers and grandfathers did. Only loyalty keeps them here."

"But they're not fighters," Martin pointed out. "Not with guns and knives. Alvarado has no less than three gunmen working for him. The rest are mean. They know how to cause trouble and enjoy killing; it doesn't matter if it's man or beast."

Filipe and Santiago shared a look. Likely, this was an old argument between them. Santiago looked down at his empty glass and sighed.

"We know," he said. "But we can't fight on those terms. We do not have the money, and it's not right."

"Not right to defend what's ours? Or ourselves?" Filipe sat forward; his eyes aflame.

Santiago was silent as he continued staring down into the glass. When he looked up, it was into Martin's eyes.

"Filipe doesn't know what war was like," Santiago said slowly. "From the scars you carry, I believe you do. I fought against Santa Ana at San Jacinto, and I don't want this land bloodied by violence."

A pregnant silence fell over them as Santiago awaited an answer. Martin saw that in his eyes, but he struggled to put it into words.

"Respectfully, *señor*," Martin said. "I only half agree with you."

Santiago's eyebrows lifted a fraction. "Why is that?"

Martin took a deep breath before continuing. "Well, when two sides have a disagreement, they settle it according to the terms of the side with the most advantage. Sometimes that's by simple talk, but most often, there's no alternative to fighting. Alvarado is no longer rational. All he wants is a fight. You've tried for many generations to settle this peacefully, and it still goes on. Only now it's getting worse. Your men have been killed for no other reason than that they traveled a public road. You can't negotiate with that, not in civil terms anyway."

"You think we should fight him with lassos and pitchforks?" Santiago sat forward; his gaze leveled with Martin's. Martin didn't look away.

"I'm saying it's time your men learned to fight with guns and knives."

For a long moment, Santiago said nothing. The conversation completely changed him from an animated storyteller to a brooding philosopher. Martin disliked the prospect of an all-out war between the two ranches as much as Santiago, but knowing Alvarado, he was confident in his words. Still, he felt a pang of shame as Santiago set his glass on the table and rose with his cane.

"I think I'll take a walk," he said. "Supper will be ready soon." He turned away and walked along the veranda. Moments later, he disappeared around the corner of the house, leaving Martin with a sinking feeling.

"Don't worry," Filipe said, reaching out to pat Martin's shoulder. "He just needs time to think. Father's been trying to convince him of the same thing for nearly a year. Grandfather always says that Father's never seen war and how it destroys land in the minds of the men that see it."

"Sometimes it has to be done," Martin muttered. He shook his head. "But that's no excuse for charging into it." He fixed Filipe with a stern look. Filipe did not hold it for long.

"He's old and tired," Filipe stated in his own defense.

"Don't value him any less for it." Martin smiled at the memory of a parlor girl in Baton Rouge who had lived to be 90. "The best thing an old man can teach a young man is how to be an old man."

Filipe said nothing. He sat, staring off into the distance. Only a few years Martin's junior, Filipe seemed a decade younger. If things went the way Martin guessed they would, Filipe would catch up quickly.

The Horse

He stood sixteen hands high, a stallion with a seal brown coat and a long, black mane and tail. His intelligent eye looked out on the world with inquisitive understanding. His black ears swiveled. One always trained on the man in the corral while the other picked up on the quiet conversation of the men on the fence.

Martin watched through the rails as Jinx waved the handle of a long carriage whip with a flag at the end and cued the horse into a trot around the circle. Martin marveled at the ease and grace of the stallion's gait, smooth and strong. Even with his somewhat limited knowledge of horses, he recognized that this was an animal to be admired. From the tones of the gathered vaqueros, he knew this was the consensus.

The horse watched Jinx as he circled, and when the man switched the whip to his other hand, the horse quickly changed direction, light on his feet as though it were all a game. After a few more turns, Jinx lowered the whip, leaning on it almost casually, and the stallion walked to him.

"He certainly knows what he's doing."

Martin looked up at Fernando. His attention had been so focused on the horse, he failed to notice Fernando's approach.

"Should you be out of the house?" Fernando asked.

Martin gave a weak smile and shook his head. "I needed to escape. Been inside too much lately."

Fernando chuckled knowingly. "Alright. Just be careful not to overdo it."

Martin nodded and watched as Jinx played an odd game with the stallion. The horse nickered in what seemed like laughter.

"Jinx has trained all our best horses," Fernando said as he leaned against the rail beside Martin. "This one he's trying to train for all uses, but I think he's a fool."

"Why?"

Fernando pointed. "That horse has a fighting streak in him. He doesn't like everybody. Last week he threw Paco quicker than a sneeze just because he could."

"Is that what Paco said?"

Fernando looked at him with a frown of thought. "Yes." He shook his head. "The point is, he's unpredictable. The only man he's not thrown yet has been Jinx, probably because he's spent so much time training him."

As they spoke, Martin watched Jinx untie the halter rope from around the stallion's neck and loop it around to the other side. The tall cowboy had no trouble vaulting onto the bareback. The stallion stood still without even shifting his weight.

"You crazy, cowpoke!" a man yelled from the other side of the corral. "He'll buck you quicker than he bucked Paco!"

"Pay them no attention, boy," Martin heard Jinx say to the horse. "Just do like I taught you."

With the lightest of signals, Jinx turned the horse back around into a circle and raised him to a trot, then crossed the corral, shifting direction in a tight figure eight, all the while flapping the whip near the horse's head.

The stallion paid no attention to the whip, or the hoots of the men as Jinx worked him. He slowed to a walk and stopped at the center. Jinx turned him in a tight circle. The stallion bent his body willingly in a dance that raised dust from the hard-packed earth. Then they went back to the circle, only this time, as they crossed the corral, they did it sideways. Martin had seen such maneuvers performed by cavalry riders. The stallion executed them with a precision that surpassed the best cavalry horse Martin had ever seen.

Off to his right, Martin heard Paco chuckle.

"I'll make him buck."

Martin looked over in time to see Paco draw and fire his revolver into the dirt. The crack and whine as the bullet bounced and flew past the horse was enough to make the other men duck, but the horse went on almost casually and only stopped at Jinx's signal. The stallion looked at Paco with an expression akin to puzzlement.

Jinx slid from the stallion's back, walked over to the fence, and stared up at Paco's grinning face. Then, in the blink of an eye, he grabbed Paco and hauled him to the dirt, pummeling him in a rolling brawl.

As the other men descended into the corral to break up the fight, the stallion looked over at Martin; ears pointed straight at him. With an almost casual gait, he walked over and stretched out his nose for a curious sniff. Martin offered his hand through the rails and felt the stallion's warm breath on his fingers. Then the stallion stepped closer, and Martin stroked his tan muzzle. By the time the fight had run its course, and the two combatants separated, the stallion had turned sideways to the corral fence and remained firmly planted by Martin. As quiet descended, the stallion looked at them with lazy humor.

The men shook their heads and walked away, some throwing up their hands as though waving away the animal's insult. Jinx stood alone, puzzling over what he saw. Finally, he picked up his hat and walked over to the horse.

"Just came over here all by his self, did he?"

Martin nodded. "I'm new, and he's the curious type."

Jinx shook his head. "No. He doesn't do that with new people." He untied the halter lead. "Come in here. I want to see what he does."

Martin walked around to the gate, not trusting his still weak limbs to climb the fence, and stepped inside as Jinx again tied the dangling lead loosely around the stallion's neck. Then he picked up the whip and handed it to Martin.

"Can you take that sling off?"

Martin hesitated before reaching behind his neck and untying the knot. As the sling came loose, he moved his arm with care. His shoulder still hurt from Kell's lazily aimed bullet, but he had seen and guessed what Jinx would have him do. He reckoned it wouldn't cause any harm. He tucked the sling in his back pocket and took the whip.

"Run him in a circle."

Knowing the look he gave Jinx was more question than confidence, Martin felt suddenly stupid, but Jinx just nodded toward the horse and said nothing.

Deliberately, Martin moved toward the stallion, flicking the flag at the end of the whip and pointing the direction with his weak arm.

The stallion responded readily and moved out, picking up pace with each hard flick of the flag.

"Change his direction."

Martin winced at the pain in his shoulder as he moved the whip from one hand to the other, but the stallion turned without missing a step.

"Call him in."

He lowered the whip, and the stallion slowed, and though he stood next to Jinx, the stallion came to Martin and lowered his head. Martin scratched his forelock of long, coarse, black hair as Jinx had, and the stallion nudged him before tossing his head.

Jinx watched them, stroking his beard in deep contemplation.

"Hope you don't intend for me to ride him," Martin said. "Don't know if my shoulder will take it."

"No." Jinx shook his head. "Not today, but you will ride him." He stepped forward and reached out to stroke the stallion's sleek, mottled neck. "I'm a firm believer that for every rider there's a horse, and for every horse, there's a rider. The choosing is as much by the one as the other. You understand?"

Martin nodded.

"Haze here has just chosen you. If Mister Fernando agrees, he's yours." He looked past Martin to Fernando, standing forgotten outside the gate.

Fernando's mouth thinned in a satisfied half-smile.

"Since you lost your horse because of my son, I believe it would be a fair trade."

"No." Martin shook his head. "I don't know the worth of horses, but a blind man can tell this one is worth much more than the one I had."

"Consider it a favor to me then," Fernando countered. "Jinx already has three horses of his own, and no one else can ride that one."

Martin gritted his teeth. He could not deny he wanted the stallion, but it was a gift greater than any he had received before in his life. He knew it was not a fair exchange.

Fernando, though, took his silence as acceptance. He pushed off the corral fence.

"See that he gets the loan of a saddle and bridle."

"Sure thing, boss."

Martin watched Fernando walk back to the house, his hand absently stroking the stallion's cheek. He had no words to express his gratitude and so remained silent.

"You know," Jinx said into the silence as he untied the lead rope again. "When that gun went off, I just about jumped out of my skin. The only two that didn't were you and this horse. That tells me he rightfully belongs to you." Jinx took the whip and handed Martin the rope. Martin took it, still saying nothing. Jinx chuckled. "Just goes to show sparsely worded folk got no business among people. Let's go put him in the corral."

Martin lingered where he was looking the stallion in the eye. He couldn't help the sense that the horse expressed understanding, as though this animal understood him better than any human he knew. For the first time in his memory, Martin felt comfortable, confident, and strong.

"Well, I reckon," he said and led Haze from the corral.

The Coming Storm

At Santiago's request, Martin continued to take his meals with the Terraza family. He felt like an intruder at first, despite the efforts of Lucia and Maricruz to make him welcome. His increasing independence drew more and more motherly criticism from Lucia. Upon learning about what happened at the corral, she scolded him for removing his sling and risking new injuries.

"What if you bled again?" she demanded. "What if you fainted, and that horse stepped on you?"

"Men don't faint, mother," Maricruz defended. "Besides, I think Martin's been on his own long enough to know what he can and cannot do."

Lucia gave a feminine scoff, eyeing her daughter with exasperation. Then she turned her piercing gaze on Martin, who raised his hand as though to ward off further onslaught.

"I'm fine, ma'am, really."

"Yes, darling," Fernando put in. "Martin wastes more strength keeping you from spoiling him."

The livid indignation rising in Lucia's face drew smiles from her husband and Santiago and left Martin fighting to not make eye contact lest he further draw her ire. Even Filipe and Maricruz seemed on the verge of laughing. Lucia looked around at them, and their brimming mirth settled her temper. She shook her head.

"Oh, you!" She waved her delicate hand at them. "All of you! You're enough to drive a woman insane." She giggled, rendering her words into a joke.

"Don't worry, dear," Fernando said with perfectly feigned seriousness. "You're not far from going loco."

Her eyes flashed a mock warning at him.

"Keep that up," Santiago told Fernando. "And I'll give you one guess where you'll be sleeping tonight."

Lucia blushed but said nothing as the two kitchen maids cleared the table. Then she pushed back her chair, signaling her departure.

"Well, if you'll excuse me," she said with deliberately exaggerated elegance. "I believe I'll take the air before retiring for the night. Maricruz, you will join me?"

Maricruz glanced up at Martin as she rose from the chair beside him.

"Will you walk with us, Martin?" she asked, blinking her soft eyelashes. She was a beautiful girl, and after the roughness of so many working women, Martin craved her company. Before he could accept her offer, Santiago spoke up.

"We have some things to discuss, Mari," he said firmly. "Maybe later."

"Meaning 'no.'" She fixed her grandfather with the look of a young woman used to getting her way and frustrated by her grandfather's denial.

Santiago's eyebrows rose in a facial shrug. Then his eyes narrowed gravely.

Maricruz's lips thinned. Had she been less disciplined, she would have stomped her foot and stormed out. Instead, she gave a single nod, like a bow first to Santiago, then to Martin.

"Perhaps later," she said, smiling wanly up at Martin.

"Yes, senorita." Martin bowed in return.

She stepped past him, and her light perfume reached him. Though it was pleasant, it failed to heat his blood.

His attention shifted to Fernando, who was helping Filipe. Santiago led them into the parlor, where he poured brandy into plain glasses. After Filipe settled into a chair beside the fireplace, Fernando set about packing his pipe. The silence continued well past the time it took them to settle in. When Santiago finally broke it, his tone sounded pained.

"I've thought about what you said yesterday, Martin, and I've concluded you're right."

Fernando stared at his father through a plume of smoke, unmoving. Filipe's eyes widened with excitement.

"Good, now we can do something about Alvarado."

"Take it easy, Filipe," Martin counseled. "Your grandfather struggled with this decision for a good reason." He looked over at the younger man. "It's nothing to celebrate."

Filipe sobered under this gentle scolding. He sat back in his chair and looked from Martin to his grandfather.

"What do you propose we do?" Fernando asked, looking at Santiago.

Santiago thought for a moment while he sipped his brandy.

"Until now," he said at last. "We've tolerated them on our land. No more. We've turned the other cheek each time Alvarado has struck. Now we stand. Our men will have to learn to fight, not just shoot and defend themselves whenever necessary." Santiago looked at Martin. "You fought in the war. Would you teach the men what you know?"

Martin met Santiago's gaze. Something about accepting made him feel dirty. It would make him no different from men like Kell. It would make him too much like the raiders during the war. Men who killed for profit wore that mark to the grave. It was a reputation he didn't want.

What was worse, he would train men to fight against his grandfather. For that reason alone, his mark should be especially indelible, but as he looked from Fernando to Santiago, he realized it was different for one reason. These men were asking his help to defend their homes and families, not make a profit, or exact revenge. Knowing that, he believed he could reconcile his conscience to what came.

"I'll help you on one condition," Martin said. "I'll work here as an ordinary hand and earn the same pay."

"That's reasonable," Fernando said with a nod. "I can understand that."

"Your men already know how to shoot. They just need to learn how to move in a fight, but ultimately, we won't know whether they'll stand until the day they face a fight." Martin saw Santiago's agreeing nod. He sat forward, leaving his drink untouched on the table. "The best I can do is teach them what I know and prepare them for the unexpected as best I can. I won't lead them in raids or any other such thing. If it comes to anything like a war, we'll deal with it as such when the time comes."

"And if the time is now?" Filipe asked.

"It's not, I'm sure of that," Martin said. "As you know, Alvarado is the last to carry the name. Once he is gone, the fight may leave those who remain."

"What if it doesn't?" Fernando asked.

"Then we'll have gained an upper hand, and they might negotiate." He looked at Santiago, hoping he had gained approval.

Fernando puffed on his pipe. "There is a rumor that Alvarado has found an heir. What do you know of that?"

Martin's heart sank. He forgot that word traveled even between enemies.

"I know Alvarado will not pass his land to another generation."

"Perhaps." Fernando's gaze lifted from the bowl of his pipe, and he gazed knowingly at Martin.

"What do you mean, Father?" Filipe asked with a frown of deep confusion.

Fernando's gaze didn't waver. "What do you think I mean, Martin?"

Martin's heart raced. He could feel the pulse of it in his wounds. He sank back in his chair and looked to Santiago for guidance, but the old man seemed equally puzzled.

"Martin?"

The words took an effort to say. All strength had gone from him, but he drew a steadying breath and spoke without pride.

"Luis Alvarado claims he's my grandfather."

Filipe's expression hardened. Anger showed through.

"You're the heir to the Alvarado estate?"

"Not anymore." Martin shook his head.

"Not anymore? You don't just stop being an Alvarado! His blood runs in your veins!"

"As it runs in yours, Filipe," Santiago stated calmly.

"But with the promise of that much land, what else could be his motivation other than to trap us? His intentions here cannot be..."

The sharp rap of Santiago's cane against the hearth silenced Filipe.

"Keep your tongue!" The old man rose and stood over Filipe, and at that moment, Martin did not doubt the danger he promised. "You are a Terraza! No Terraza has shown ingratitude as you have just now!"

Silence fell. Martin's chest felt tight. All the while, he felt Fernando watching him.

Santiago's attention remained focused on Filipe. He waved his hand at Martin.

"You owe this man your *life*. Such ungracious behavior has no place here."

Martin dared not look up as Santiago retreated to his chair and sank into it.

"Whatever proof Luis has I say is false," Santiago declared. "Martin is no grandson of his."

"Are you sure, Father?" Fernando asked pointedly. "You know what it will cost us if you're wrong."

Santiago stared at his son for a long time. Then his gaze shifted to Martin. Unlike those times when Alvarado studied him, Martin felt at ease, as though everything was right in the world. Santiago gave a confident nod.

"I am sure."

This seemed to satisfy Fernando. He nodded in return and sat back to smoke his pipe in silence.

For a long while, none of them spoke. Though Martin felt uneasy in the quiet, he feared speaking might break open a new flood of anger.

"I don't like it," Santiago finally said. "But I will accept that the time has come." He leveled his gaze at Martin again. "I hope you will help us with this. I believe what you have told me of your quest to find your family, your home, and I believe you will help us with good intentions."

Again, Martin felt the reassurance of Santiago's trust. "Shall we start tomorrow?"

Santiago shook his head adamantly. "*Mañana es Domingo*." He rose. "We'll not taint a holy day with such things." He rose from the velvet armchair. "I am sorry to retire so early, but this discussion has used the last of my strength."

"Good night, father," Fernando said as Santiago hobbled past him. Unlike his normal self, Santiago did not reply. Martin felt something sink inside him.

Once Santiago was gone, Fernando went to the hearth and knocked the embers out of his pipe. "We should retire as well. It is a long ride to Mass." He looked at Martin. "You are welcome to join us."

Martin couldn't remember the last time he'd been to a church service. The idea of attending made him uneasy, but he thanked Fernando out of courtesy.

Fernando put away his pipe. Filipe rose and seemed to hesitate.

"I'm sorry for what I said."

Martin gazed up at him and smiled to show Filipe he forgave him. "I understand. I only hope I will defend my family with the same determination as you."

"Thank you," Filipe said sincerely.

Fernando took Filipe's arm. "Will you sit up a while, Martin?"

Martin nodded, his mind too agitated to sleep. "Until the fire dies."

Fernando nodded. "Good night to you."

Fernando and Filipe disappeared down the hall, leaving Martin alone.

For a long while, he sat staring into the flames, slowly sipping the brandy Santiago had poured for him. He welcomed the calm the spirit brought his body and mind, though he did not savor the sensation. Too many things weighed on him. Chiefly, it was Santiago's insistence that Alvarado was not Martin's grandfather. Did Santiago know more than he was telling in the long stories of his youth? Perhaps his was the same path as so many young men leading from the bed of one woman to the next. Martin shook his head at the thought, believing Santiago too loyal, even in years past, to be so fickle. Still, he could be wrong. Likely, Santiago knew of a family whose daughter had fled home with her infant son but bore no relation to them.

Martin drew a deep breath and sighed. He drained the last of the brandy from his glass. He could sit for hours and wonder or ask Santiago why he was so confident. However, tonight was not a good night to ask the question. It would have to wait for a better time.

Returning the glass to the sideboard, Martin turned down the lamp and paused for a moment, watching the fingers of flame play over the coals in the hearth. Somehow, it reminded him of the fragility of the world and how easily faith, trust, reputation, and life itself could change direction with a breath of air. How quickly the direction of his own life had changed! Thankful it had changed for the better, he turned away from the hearth and followed the line of windows down the hall to his room.

Heat shimmered against the distant buttes in a phantasmal dance between dry earth and cloudless sky. From the top of a ravine, Martin sat and watched. The brown stallion fidgeted, discontented with stillness.

"Settle down, boy," Martin advised. "Won't be here much longer."

The spring was to the south. It promised work, clearing out silt that had fallen in during the spring rains, but for the moment, he was content to sit and watch the landscape. Twenty feet away, a rattlesnake stirred.

Aware of the animal, Martin made no move against it, but glanced in its direction occasionally. Sensing something too big to eat, the snake flicked its tongue and crawled toward the edge where it disappeared into the rocks.

The land was beautiful and dangerous, like the landscape of the human mind with the ability to dream of things that could be and possess the horrors of the past at the same time. Through the months since he left Alvarado's employ, he walked carefully among the Terraza family and their ranch hands. Martin stayed away from town, intent on avoiding Kell and the others in the hope of making a new life among the Terrazas. He always rode with someone to avoid rumors he remained in contact with Alvarado. He rode alone today only because Fernando sent him out despite Martin's insistence that another man accompany him. The other hands attended their own tasks, and so Martin rode west, away from Alvarado land, and savored his first time without another human in sight in many months. He could have remained on this bluff all day, basking in the sun and the heat, but work waited.

"Alright, boy, let's go."

The horse turned along the edge, and Martin searched for the trail down. As he rode, his mind wandered to Lolita. He had not thought of her in the last two months, and for a moment, he wondered if she was well. A powerful urge to ride to Alvarado's ranch to find out came over him. He shook his head and felt a pang of guilt for abandoning her.

Halfway down the slope, he noticed the tracks of another horse. He paused and studied them. In the time he spent with Jinx, riding, and learning how to train horses, he also learned to read their tracks. This trail looked familiar. Teasing at the memory, he failed to recall it and continued down toward the spring.

The air turned sour with the smell of rot a quarter mile from the spring. Haze hesitated, sniffing the wind.

"I smell it too, boy." He patted the sleek neck reassuringly. "Let's find out what it is."

Picking his way through the juniper along a narrow cattle trail, Haze expressed his concern with a soft nicker. Martin felt the same unease and worried they might stumble across a dead man from either side of the boundary. The thought turned his stomach.

As they rounded a bend in the trail and came into view of the waterhole, Martin felt relief at the sight of a dead deer beside the earthen dam, but the feeling evaporated at the question of why it died.

Dismounting several feet from the water source, Martin tied Haze to a stout juniper and approached cautiously, watching the rocks above.

But the deer had no marks, only a swollen tongue and glazed eyes. Not even buzzards had descended upon the young buck. Looking up at the water, Martin understood why. Another deer, bloated by the heat radiating off the rocks, lay at the water's edge just above the earthen wall. No cat stalked this place. It was the water, likely poisoned by human hands. Like so many others in the area, this water hole was dug out and dammed into troughs by the early Spanish settlers and had provided water for hundreds of generations of cattle and wild game. Before now, the water from this spring had always run sweet.

Going back to his horse, Martin took out the shovel. On the low side of the dam, he dislodged the stones and dirt until the pressure of the water broke through and washed down into the gully below. He scrambled to higher ground and watched the leading tide uproot and wash away tufts of grass as it went. In a day or two, he would return with others to rebuild the dam. For now, it would have to drain and dry.

"Sorry, boy, no cool water for you." He tied the shovel behind his saddle and took down his canteen, still half-filled from the morning. He gave the stallion a share and took a little for himself. Then he mounted and turned Haze back toward the trail, but the horse shied, refusing to go forward. His ears perked toward the brush, and Martin felt his skin crawl. He was in the open, exposed to anyone hidden in the juniper.

He listened hard, but the heavy silence yielded no clues. Even the songbirds perched silently in the trees.

Then, from far back along the trail, he heard the scrape of a hoof against a stone.

It could have been a cow or a deer, but Haze did not relax, and so Martin reached for his rifle, quietly opened the breech, and chambered a round. Sliding from the saddle, he ground-hitched the stallion and slipped into concealment among the junipers to wait.

The rider didn't hide his approach. Martin tracked his progress by sound and let him ride past into the clearing around the waterhole. It was then Martin recognized the white-faced sorrel.

Letting down the hammer, Martin stepped back into the clearing.

"Hello, Paco."

Paco jumped, reaching for the gun on his hip. Reflexively, Martin trained the rifle on him. When Paco saw who he was, a laugh bubbled to his lips.

"Who did you think I was?"

"Not sure." Martin lowered the rifle. "Maybe you were the one who poisoned this water hole."

"Poisoned?"

"*Sí.*"

Paco's eyebrows rose. He glanced over and saw the deer. Then he stepped down and bent to study the nearest carcass.

"Cyanide, I think," he said. "And a lot of it. Small amounts take a while to work."

Martin nodded and returned the rifle to its scabbard tucked under the right fender of his saddle. "What are you doing out here, Paco? I thought Señor Fernando sent you north this morning."

"He said for me to start around here and sweep north. Little Lupe is with me, but he didn't want to come down here."

"Why?"

Paco frowned. "Can you keep a secret?"

Martin studied him for a moment before giving a hesitant nod. Paco glanced around, then leaned in close and spoke in a conspiratorial tone.

"He doesn't like to climb hills. Neither does his horse."

Martin laughed hard and long. Despite his name, Little Lupe was one of the biggest men Martin had ever seen. He nearly passed out fighting not to laugh the first time he saw Lupe balanced on the back of a cow pony with hardly any room left for anything behind his saddle. The thought of that same under sized animal carrying the oversized man down that rock face resurrected the mirth.

"At least he has mercy," Martin said as he wiped tears from his eyes.

"*Sí.*" Paco surveyed the water hole again and shrugged. "Well, no point in staying here with no water to drink." He climbed back into the saddle and waited for Martin.

Martin let Paco lead as they climbed back to the lip of the canyon.

Little Lupe waited, reclining against the trunk of a dead scrub pine with his hat pulled down over his face. His snores rumbled through the stillness. As Martin and Paco neared, he woke with a start and rolled to his feet.

Paco called out to him, teasing him for his laziness. Lupe waved a hand at him and hauled his bulk into the saddle. Lupe told him about the waterhole.

"*Bastardos.*" Lupe spat into the dirt.

Paco scoffed in agreement. He turned his attention back to Martin. "I forgot to tell you, Señor Fernando wanted you back at the ranch. He wants you to go with the wagon for supplies tomorrow."

Martin frowned at this. The last two days, he spent out here, riding from waterhole to waterhole without seeing another soul. He liked it that way. The thought of meeting up with Kell or Armand in town sent chills through him. Protesting to Paco, however, would be pointless.

"Alright," he said. "You two take care. No telling if they didn't poison other water holes."

"*Bastardos,*" Lupe cursed again.

"*Bastardos,*" Martin agreed before he turned Haze northeast and gave him his head. The long-legged horse reached out in an easy lope that devoured the miles in a few hours. The supper hour neared when he rode through the south gate.

Seated in his usual spot on the porch, Santiago waved and called for him to come over. His expression was sedate and inviting. If Martin could wish for a grandfather, Santiago was such a man. Even on days when his worn body hurt from age, Santiago smiled graciously and offered thanks for every bit of kindness showed him, and for the simple blessing of being alive.

Martin tied Haze out of reach of the flower bed, but the stallion tried for the roses anyway and flinched when he stuck his soft muzzle on the thorns.

"That should teach you," Martin scolded. He tugged off his gloves and tucked them in his belt as he stepped through the little iron gate. His greeting Santiago in Spanish and the old man's expression brightened. The language returned to him bit by bit over the past months, and he felt a sense of pride at cheering Santiago with the words.

"Sit. Talk to me." There were two glasses on the table, and Santiago filled the second with cool water before he offered it to Martin.

Sinking into the chair on the far side of the table, Martin stretched his legs with a thankful sigh. The cool shade was welcome on his tanning face. He drank deeply of the water and smiled at its sweetness.

For a while, silence hung in the air. Santiago stared down into his still full glass, his face pale and his hands restless. Something bothered him, and this worried Martin.

"What do you wish to talk about?" Martin finally asked.

Santiago opened his mouth to speak and seemed to lose the words. Several moments passed before he attempted again. His voice was soft and almost fearful. "I do not believe you told me why your mother left her family."

Martin sipped the water, sweet and cool. He told Santiago his brief story several weeks before in a poor return for the rich history of the Terraza family. This last remained unspoken because of Maricruz and her excitement over a new dress. Now, asked to tell it, Martin felt reluctant, but he drew a fortifying breath and spoke.

"After my father was killed, my grandmother wanted Mother to remarry to a man she didn't love. When Mother refused, my grandmother disowned her."

Santiago's attention drifted to the garden. He was silent for a long moment, then asked. "What of your grandfather?"

"Mother said he was a kind man, and gentle, too gentle with my grandmother. She said she left because she could no longer live with what my grandmother expected." He studied Santiago as he spoke. The old man's gaze was distant, thoughtful, and haunted. Excitement stirred in Martin's breast with a rise in hope, but he kept his tone neutral. "Why do you ask?"

Santiago shook his head and smiled wanly. "No reason." He glanced over at Martin and changed the topic. "I see you're not wearing a gun like the other young men. Even Filipe has one."

Martin let the conversation take its turn. He would await another chance.

"The rifle is good enough," Martin said with conviction.

"But it is wise to keep a weapon close to hand in times like these," Santiago countered.

"It also invites trouble where it would not come otherwise." Martin stared grimly at the little fountain a few feet away, puzzling over how to ask Santiago the question he needed answered. When Santiago did not say more, he pushed forward. "Santiago, what do you know of my parents?"

A look of pain washed over the old man's face, betraying a depth of knowledge Santiago did not wish to dredge.

"Must you ask such a question?" Santiago stared past the fountain with a weary, distant gaze.

"Yes, sir. That's why I came to this country."

Slowly, painfully, the old man nodded. He understood, but even as his lips parted to form words, his voice remained silent. Twice he started to speak. Both times, he failed, adding to Martin's frustration. Despite it, Martin forgave the old man who had proven that few things were so hard for him. It was harder for him to reconcile himself with knowing that the truth was there, just out of reach and that his love for the old man prohibited him from causing Santiago any more sadness.

"Perhaps another time," Martin said, finishing the glass of water and rising. "Soon?"

Santiago's gaze lifted from the fountain. He blinked as though returning to the present. Whatever memories Martin's question unlocked were strong, and Martin felt a pang of guilt for bringing them to the surface. But Santiago smiled and bowed his head gratefully.

"Yes," Santiago said. "It will be soon. I promise."

Martin reached out and rested his hand on Santiago's shoulder. Then he retreated down the path through the gate. Haze gave him a confused look as he untied the lead rope. Rose thorns had scratched small tracks of blood over his delicate nose.

"For an animal with so much brains, you're awfully slow sometimes," Martin said and led Haze toward the corral. He glanced back at Santiago, who still stared into the distance. Martin wondered if asking the favor of reaching for the moon would have been an easier task for Santiago.

"Patience is a skill upon which all other skills are built," his mother once told him as a child.

"You never said how hard patience would be, Mother," Martin whispered. But he knew now that such a thing was hard to teach a child. Silencing his own impatience, he unsaddled Haze and found other chores to fill his time until supper.

Cowards

"Damn you, José!" Jinx unfastened the harness on the big black mare. "How many times've I got to tell you not to twist these? It rubs the poor animal raw."

"*Lo siento, señor*." The boy hung his head, thoroughly crestfallen at his failure to harness the horse to Jinx's standards.

Jinx stared at him with a mix of pity and frustration. "It ain't hard. You just got to remember. Look here."

Martin crossed his arms and leaned against the wagon wheel as he watched Jinx show the boy again how to run the harness, but the damage had already been done. The boy looked too dejected to focus on what the old horseman told him. When Jinx dismissed him, José turned to leave and saw Martin's empathetic face.

"I tried, *señor*," he said.

"*Si.*" Martin patted the boy's shoulder and told him he would learn with time, then sent him away to his chores.

"You go too easy on that boy," Jinx said when José had disappeared beyond the barn.

"He's a little slower than most," Martin said. "He doesn't do it out of spite."

"True." Jinx took up the reins and released the brake. "But I still wish he'd pay attention when I talk."

The wagon jostled forward. As they pulled onto the road, Martin glanced back and saw Jose standing by the stable door, watching them. It reminded Martin of something, but the memory remained out of reach of his recollection.

"How's Haze working for you?"

"Very well. He's a good horse."

"That he is!" Jinx declared proudly. He leaned forward, rested his elbows on his knees, and held the reins loosely in his gnarled hands. "You know I've heard a few things, rumors really," he mused.

"What rumors?"

"Like why Santiago wanted to keep you around."

Martin shook his head, feeling sick at the prospect of dredging up the topic. "I don't want to talk about it."

Jinx held up a hand. "Now hear me out. I've worked for the Terrazas for a long time. I started here when I was no more than fifteen. I'm almost forty now, and my memory's good. My memory for faces is better than the rest of the old-timers."

"What are you getting at?" Martin asked after a long silence. Jinx did not reply immediately, making Martin uneasy. Martin wanted answers, but he doubted he wanted to hear them from Jinx.

Jinx's jaw flexed. "Santiago had a daughter. Fair-haired, with the most beautiful eyes you ever saw. Green and gold, they were!" He let out a whistle, marveling at the memory. "Tried to catch her fancy myself when I was about your age, but she had eyes for another man. He was an American from back east somewhere. A gentleman of sorts, looking for a new life." He chuckled and shook his head. "When I first saw him, he was still wearing what had been a fine suit of clothes, worn by travel. He was a big man, tall and strong. That man could outfight any man who dared try him. He had two sons. Both, I imagine, grew to be like their pa. Identical twins, they were. Those two got into a tussle with some of the boys around the ranch. Outnumbered six to two, and dang it, they won! Looked like hell when it was over, but they won."

Martin frowned inwardly and felt worn. The last thing he wanted was another ploy to win his loyalty, or another story to pass the time, but Jinx seemed disinclined toward silence. Gritting his teeth, he decided to keep the conversation going for no other reason than to get his mind off the whole thing. "I don't follow you. What's this got to do with Santiago's daughter?"

"I'm getting to that." Jinx waved his hand. "Where was I? Oh, yeah. Well, this feller started playing for Miss Izzy's affections. When he went to ask permission, Santiago refused." He shrugged and played with the reins. "We all guessed it was really the old woman who said 'no.' She hated gringos with a passion. My wife once told me she wished them all dead."

"I still don't see the point of this."

Jinx glared benignly. "If you'd hold y'er tongue and listen, I'll get to the point."

Martin sighed and pretended to listen. Before long, Jinx's rhythmic tone wore him down, and he wanted to sleep, but he watched the road, only distantly aware of the man's ramblings. When they reached the outskirts of town, Martin felt the back of his neck tingle.

The Alvarado's supply wagon was hard to miss. Painted red from seat to wheels, it stood out against the white adobe of the grocery. Jinx fell silent, and his keen eyes swept the street. Martin glanced back for any sign of the driver. He guessed Lolita drove the wagon, as was her usual routine. Then he saw Armand step out of the cantina. Kell and Chico stepped out and flanked him, hands hanging loosely at their sides.

"Keep going," Martin advised. Jinx nodded and flicked the reins.

They rolled up to the gunsmith's shop and stopped. Before Martin could think what to do, Jinx climbed down to the boardwalk.

"Stay with the wagon," Jinx ordered as he looped the reins around the brake leaver. "I'll only be a minute."

Martin nodded. "They probably think they're seeing a ghost." He glanced back at the three men. Kell and Chico were talking, but Armand's attention rested solely on Martin. Lines of anger covered his face.

Despite the summer sun, Martin felt a chill, yet he held Armand's gaze until the other man looked away. Armand stepped off the boardwalk and started across the street toward the Alvarado wagon. Casting a deliberate sideways glance at Martin, Armand strode past the wagon and into the grocer's store.

Climbing down to the boardwalk, Martin watched Kell and Chico lounge in front of the saloon, eyeing him in bitter silence. Martin wanted a gun in his hand if, for no other reason than to reassure himself, he was not helpless this time, but the act of reaching for the rifle under the wagon seat could touch off the brewing fight.

A while later, Jinx stepped out of the shop and placed a large, paper-wrapped package under the seat.

"They ain't left yet?" he asked

"No, but they know I'm here. Not sure if it shook them up or just primed them for a fight."

"Either way, I hope two things." Jinx spit tobacco juice between the wagon wheels. "I hope they finish up and leave, or they do something foolish."

Martin swallowed and prayed for the former. He harbored no love for either Armand or Kell, but he remembered Chico's plea to spare him the bullet when he and Kell dumped him in the wash. Though Chico had not been what Martin considered a friend, he was not a true enemy either.

"Wish we could have a drink," Jinx commented as he leaned against the wagon.

Martin had no desire for alcohol or even water. While part of him wanted a fight, another feared it. He didn't fear death, but the implications of a full fight. A fight started today would end as a bloodbath between the two ranches. He took a deep breath and tried to calm his quivering nerves.

"Bastards," Jinx hissed.

Down the street, a woman shrieked in Spanish. She stumbled suddenly from the grocery and fell against the wheel of Alvarado's supply wagon. Martin squinted and recognized Lolita's familiar form.

Heat flooded Martin, and he started for Lolita as Armand grabbed her and shoved her against the wheel. Jinx caught Martin's arm.

"Don't, son! He's trying to goad you into it!"

Martin fought him. Jinx surprised him with a burst of strength as he shoved Martin into the mercantile wall.

"You do this; you'll touch off a full war!" Jinx hissed in Martin's ear.

"No one deserves to be treated like that!" Martin lunged, and Jinx slammed him against the wall again.

"Fool! You aren't even wearing a gun. Armand will shoot you like a dog. He's probably looking for an excuse, as it is."

Martin stilled, knowing that Jinx was right. Even with that realization, Martin hated the sudden wash of cowardice that overcame him. He watched as Lolita spat at Armand. With a gloved hand, Armand reached up and wiped the spit from his cheek, then slapped her across the face. Again, Martin tried to break free.

"Armand won't kill her. She's too valuable to him alive. Think about all the men that will die if you do this!"

Jinx's words had a sobering effect. The images of countless dead scattered over fields and through forests passed before Martin's eyes. It brought back the old sickness and a new, helpless ache.

Martin's body relaxed as Lolita, ever defiant, tossed the hair back from her face, holding her head high. Then she climbed into the wagon with a flip of her skirt. Armand climbed up beside her and took up the reins. Only then did Jinx relax his hold.

Martin picked up his hat and stood staring after the wagon as Armand reined the horses into the street and passed by at a trot. Kell and Chico followed on horseback and drew up where Martin and Jinx stood.

"You saw that, Gray Boy?" Kell demanded. "That's what he'll do again if we see your carcass again." His attention shifted to Jinx, and he leveled a finger at Martin. "Tell your friends back home if they bring him to Alvarado dead, there's a lot of land in it for them."

Martin felt Jinx stiffen beside him. He knew he should feel fear, sharp and sickening. Instead, he felt rage. What stayed his hand was the knowledge that the rifle was too far away to give him a decent chance of killing Kell.

Kell grinned with the same enjoyment as he did the day he killed the roan mare after she threw him into the fence. "Yeah, Alvarado says you're his sole heir, and if you won't have his land, the man who kills you can."

A strange calm came over Martin. The door to his future had shut, and he had no regrets about walking away.

He filled his lungs and spoke with confidence. "Then tell Alvarado I have no use for him. I want no part of a family like his."

Again, that grin, like a Gila monster sunning himself, sent rage through Martin. Kell leaned down and said to Martin alone.

"By the end of this, you will want Alvarado's favor. The only way you get out of this is if you bring the bodies of every Terraza to him. Your only other choice is a slow, painful death."

The battle fever rose in Martin again, and his face betrayed him. Kell saw it and laughed out loud as he jerked his horse's head around and laid spurs to her flanks. The horse screamed and leaped into a dead run to catch up to the wagon.

Chico held back. His expression betrayed shame.

"Tell the others not to come to town again," Chico told Jinx. "Señor Alvarado has ordered any Terraza rider to be shot on sight unless they have Martin's body with them." When his attention shifted from Jinx, but he could not meet Martin's gaze. "I'm very sorry."

Martin studied the Tejano's face. Unlike the others, Chico genuinely hated bloodshed. Perhaps it was the loss of his mother to Comancheros in his childhood, but regret at what lay ahead showed plainly in his eyes. Martin nodded in forgiveness.

The gesture did little to ease Chico's conscience. His expression resembled that of a beaten dog as he turned his horse and rode away at an easy trot.

"Makes you think, don't it?" Jinx asked, stepping to the edge of the walk beside Martin. "All that land, good land too. And all you have to do is kill a few people. Hell, you could slit their throats while they sleep."

Indeed, Martin could. He lost count of the men he killed that way during the war, but the Terrazas had been kind to him, something he valued far more highly than land. He asked himself if he could kill them to save his life. Each one he considered, and to each one his heart and mind responded with an unwavering "no," leaving him with two choices. Stay and face certain death or flee and be hunted for the rest of his life.

Martin's attention shifted to the saloon across the street. Suddenly, a drink of whiskey sounded good. It was foolish, he knew, but Fate rarely favored him anyway, and he was tired of fighting her. Martin started across the street without a word to Jinx.

Santiago climbed into the carriage and sat back comfortably on the leather seat. Paco latched the door and climbed onto the driver's seat. He flicked the reins, starting the pair of lean bays out onto the road. Santiago watched the land roll past and smiled at the memories it recalled. Here he spent his childhood wandering among the brush in search of lizards and rocks of different shapes and colors. Here, he played and learned the value and fragility of life. In the hills and prairies far to the east, he had fought beside the Texans against Santa Ana and learned what killing and death truly meant. He went to war an idealist with only dreams and came home fragile with a new idealism. Here in this land, he had fallen in love and helped create life, his effort too small a token to make up for his sins against life. In his mind, his children had grown into good people despite his deficiencies as a father and husband.

As the carriage pulled into the yard of the old mission, he remembered again his wedding and how that single day changed his life forever and set the course of events that now unfurled.

Carmelita had been a beautiful woman, but demanding and proud to a fault. Never could he fully satisfy her desires for prestige and fashion. Only after years did he finally learn of her hatred for the Americans who moved to Texas and drove out the Spanish. To her, Texas belonged to Spain and always should. Even the taint of Santiago's mestizo blood drew her disdain. By the time he learned this, it was too late.

Paco opened the door and offered a steady hand as Santiago climbed from the carriage.

"Water the horses and wait here," Santiago told him. "I'll be an hour at most."

"*Si, señor*." Paco bowed his head respectfully.

Inside the old mission chapel, the air was cool and carried a faint scent of damp earth, which seeped up through the stone floor. The narrow windows offered little light. In the shadows around the altar, candles flickered and danced like so many souls burning in purgatory, suffering their final penance before entering Heaven.

Santiago knelt at the communion rail, laid down his cane, and prayed as he had prayed for so many years, only now, instead of pleading for his only daughter's health and return, he prayed for her soul and for the soul of her only son.

The old, black-robed priest stepped out of the vestibule, genuflected stiffly, and retired to the confessional as he always did upon Santiago's arrival.

Heart pounding with a fear he had not known since he was a young man, Santiago signed himself and took up his cane. He made his way behind the partition, his footsteps echoing against the high ceiling.

"Have you come to confess, Santiago?" the priest asked.

"Yes, father. I apologize that my confession today will be long."

He saw the priest's eyebrow rise through the lattice dividing the cells of the confessional. For years this routine had been familiar to both of them, and while they had often discussed philosophy for hours, never had Santiago's confessions taken more than a few minutes. The priest's reaction brought a soft chuckle from Santiago, as much to alleviate the priest's concern as to ease Santiago's fear.

"I never thought an old man could sin so much." Santiago sighed as a wave of emotion hit him. The priest said nothing, only waited with his head bowed.

"Forgive me, father, for I have sinned many times in my life. As a boy, I cared little for others and so caused them hardship and anger. I used others to gain what I wanted. Out of negligence, I caused many animals pain unnecessarily. Twelve times I took the lives of my enemies in battle, though that fact makes me no less guilty. I lusted after a woman, believing unwisely that her faults could be overlooked and made her my wife. Many times I neglected my husbandly duties and sought refuge in excess drink. I beat my children without just cause and believed lies that were told me." He paused as the full weight of guilt settled on his old shoulders. "These are my greatest sins, father, but the greatest of all is I am a coward."

Santiago reached for the words to continue as shame and anguish closed his throat. He bowed his head but could not speak.

The priest waited a moment before gently asking, "How are you a coward?"

The question gave his mind direction. Santiago reached into his pocket for his handkerchief and pressed it to his eyes, giving his throat time to open again.

"Many years ago," he said through tears. "My wife tried to force our daughter to remarry after it was believed her husband had died. She wanted Maitea to give her child away and raise a family of 'good Spanish blood.'" He bit out the words angrily and felt suddenly guilty. "Forgive me; I am as guilty as she for my lack of action against it." He paused, letting the anger dissipate. "Once, she beat Maitea's son nearly to death because he was half *Americano*. He had not yet reached his second birthday."

The priest waited in silence as Santiago sobbed quietly. When Santiago continued, his voice sounded brittle. "I did nothing to stop it. I did nothing to keep my daughter from taking the child and leaving because I believed it was for the best."

No longer could Santiago hold back the tears that, for so many years, lay ignored deep in his heart. He buried his face in his hands and wept.

The priest gazed at him through the lattice, saying nothing. When the tears eased, the priest spoke with compassion and kindness.

"Why do you confess this today? Your daughter left after I arrived twenty years ago, yet I have not heard you speak of this until now."

"Because, father, I believe with all my heart that her son has returned."

The bench creaked as the priest shifted, and understanding flashed on his face. "The young stranger who has joined your family at mass."

Santiago nodded.

Bowing his head, the priest fell deep into thought. "I remember his eyes from when I baptized him."

"Yes, father! The same gold flecks of Maitea's yes. It's a trait in my family!"

"And you have not told him of this?" The priest didn't look up, but his tone was no less probing.

"No."

"Why?"

"Alvarado has already claimed him as his own grandson. Fernando doubts me, but my memory is not weak." He paused, framing the other part of his explanation. "I fear, if I tell Martin, he will only believe me mad or that I am attempting to use him as a pawn in this absurd feud as Luis has."

The priest nodded in understanding. Then another question occurred to him. He considered it for a moment before he spoke.

"You said your daughter 'believed' her husband was dead. Was he?"

Santiago shook his head. "My wife lied to both my daughter and my son-in-law. She told each the other was dead. Then, a year before she died, a letter came from Bodie, my son-in-law, inviting us to his ranch in the north. That was when she confessed what she had done. I could not speak to her again after that." He cleared his throat, regaining his composure. "I feared her too much, as I now fear telling my grandson the truth."

"You must tell him," the priest counseled after several moments of consideration. "He deserves to know. If there is any chance left of finding his father, he should it."

"But how? How can I tell him he and his mother were driven from our home, and I did nothing to stop it? And what of Luis? What will he do to Martin if Martin accepts the truth?"

"You must tell him. You will only drive him farther away by continuing the lie."

These words struck Santiago's heart. He knew they were true and nodded assent. But how would he tell Martin the story without the young man feeling some anger toward him? Then he remembered Martin possessed his mother's compassion and his father's fighting spirit.

"Since this seems a great task for you, let it be your penance and reparation to God and your kindred."

Santiago smiled wryly. It was a fitting penance, but it weighed no less heavily on his soul. "Thank you, father," he said sincerely.

"Now go in peace, and God bless you, Santiago."

Santiago bowed his head and made the sign of the cross as the priest spoke the words of absolution.

Ghosts of Spain

They rode back to the ranch without a word spoken between them. Martin, nerves eased by several shots of tequila, stared at the land deep in thought. Jinx respectfully let him and contented himself with his own thoughts. The old *caballero* knew no one could change the young man's situation. Though Martin knew it consciously, his mind remained restless, searching for a way to change his fate.

The sun crossed the sky in white indifference and hung two hours from sliding below the horizon when they pulled into the yard. Martin climbed down and wordlessly set to unloading the wagon. Fernando appeared on the house veranda dressed in his range clothes.

"Where have you two been?" he demanded. His expression burned with anger.

"It took us a while to get everything," Jinx replied, eyes tight with concern.

Fernando jerked his head in Martin's direction. "Was he with you the whole time?"

Jinx openly frowned. "Yeah. Why? Something wrong?"

"Santiago," Fernando said, his expression softening enough to betray his worry. "He and Paco should have returned from the mission hours ago. We've heard nothing." He stared at Martin in contemplation. When he spoke, his tone sounded reluctant. "Saddle your horse. You'll ride with me."

Despite the lingering burn of liquor, Martin felt Fernando's restrained urgency. He hurried to the corral and saddled Haze. The stallion, usually playful during this process, stood still though his muscles twitched with excitement. Martin dropped the stirrup and swung up into the saddle. Fernando waited for him at the gate, astride his palomino, and they started out along the trail to the old mission ten miles distant.

Fernando was silent, and his manner forbade any word of comfort that Martin might have offered. For a moment, Martin wondered if it was pure fear for Santiago's safety or the *patrón's* suspicion of him that convinced Fernando to bring him along. In his current state, Martin cared nothing for Fernando's opinion of him. His only concern was finding Santiago and bringing him safely home.

They rode along opposite sides of the road, each watching the carriage tracks scarring the hard earth. Six miles from the ranch, Martin spotted where the trail left the road.

"*Señor!*"

He did not have to say more. Fernando's horse reached him in two long strides. His face blanched at the parallel grooves running into the brush.

"Is Paco in the habit of galloping the horses?" Martin asked after a moment.

Fernando looked at him, and Martin pointed to the ground, indicating the tracks of the horse team running side by side between the lines of carriage wheels. The man's expression darkened, and he shook his head. "Where were they going?"

Martin did not know the answer. Rising in the saddle, he traced the trail in a wide circle through the brush and back along the road toward the mission. Santiago was never in a hurry, and so Paco would not gallop the horses without purpose. The way the trail laid out, Martin guessed something made them retreat to the mission and what safety it may provide. A shock ran through Martin's veins, driving away the last of the alcohol and leaving a cold clamminess on his skin.

He turned Haze up the road and heeled him into a lope. Fernando rode close on his heels.

They were another mile closer to the mission when the trail left the road again and led down into a steep gully. The tracks did not return to the road.

There, on the edge of the drop, amid broken juniper and sage, they found the wrecked carriage. Both horses lay unmoving in their traces.

Doubt and disappointment cooled Martin's blood. He had hoped the team had made the four miles back to the mission and that he and Fernando faced the simple task of rescue. Seeing the wrecked carriage banished all hope he held. Drawing a deep breath, he started forward, ready to face the inevitable. Fernando caught his arm and held him back. Martin obeyed, knowing it was not his place to charge in and disturb the place of the dead.

It took Fernando another moment to fight back the trepidation of finding his father. When he started his horse down the slope, Martin waited and followed close behind. Once in the gully's bottom, though, Fernando's surge of bravado dissipated, and he sat his horse staring at the overturned carriage bottom. When he glanced up, his expression pleaded with Martin.

There was nothing Martin could say. He glanced at the carriage, then back at Fernando, who nodded his permission for Martin to search it.

Before he dismounted, Martin leaned over to peer inside the carriage. The only sign of Santiago was his cane lying across the far window. Climbing from the saddle onto the side of the carriage, Martin lowered himself inside, feeling with his feet lest he land on Santiago's body. Several moments passed while his eyes adjusted to the dim light. As the shapes of the seats formed out of the shadows, Martin scanned the interior. Hope re-surged in him when he found no sign of Santiago. The far door rested open against the bank. Martin kneeled and peered through it.

The coach had fallen against the bank, leaving a narrow space underneath. The crash happened with such force that both right wheels broke off the hubs, and the axles gouged into the ground, but the space was just wide enough a slight man like Santiago could have crawled through. Martin studied the ground, but the scuffs and scratches were hard to read from his angle. He saw no blood and hoped it was a good sign.

Climbing back into the sunlight, he cast a single glance at Fernando, who searched the ground near the horses. He vaulted off the carriage and walked back to where the disturbed sand showed where Santiago dragged himself from beneath the carriage into a nearby manzanita thicket. The mark of Santiago's stiff right leg was clear, but a lighter mark beside it indicated a useless right hand.

Hurried strides took Martin to the thicket where he dropped to his hands and knees and crawled into the tangle of branches.

"Santiago?" he called as the branches grabbed at his head and shoulders, but no reply came. He pushed on, heedless of the dried manzanita digging into his exposed flesh.

Then, through the haze of gray boughs, he spotted the maroon of Santiago's jacket. The old man lay curled up against the bank in the shade, his head bloody, his right arm cradled across his body.

"Fernando, over here!" Martin worked his way around to the old man's head. Gently, he turned Santiago onto his side.

The old man stirred but made no sound. His eyes opened to pain-pinched slits. It took a moment for his gaze to focus. Then relief washed over his age lined features.

"Martín." He smiled, but Martin didn't miss how the old man pronounced his name. He dismissed it as delirium from the strike to his head.

"Don't talk," Martin counseled. "I don't know how bad you're hurt." He looked the old man over then back the way he came. "Fernando!"

"Martín." There was an urgency in his voice, a plea that made Martin's heart ache. Santiago reached out and grasped Martin's arm with more strength than Martin believed the old man possessed.

"*Escucha me,*" Santiago commanded. "*Remember, you asked why I wanted to know about your mother?*"

"That can wait, *Abuelo*," Martin said, trying to calm him.

Santiago shook his head, clinging to Martin's sleeve. "*You have to know...*" His voice faltered, and he forced the words from his lips. "*You have to know the truth.*"

Martin looked up at the sound of branches snapping behind him as Fernando made his way through the thicket.

Santiago's hand grasped his collar and dragged his attention back to the old man. Martin told him to be still while he and Fernando found a way to get him out.

"No!" He stared up at Martin with a strange, gentle look on his face as he spoke in Spanish, the language of his childhood.

Torn between the denial of loss and the need to grant the old man this last request, Martin's mind wrestled with the meaning of what Santiago told him. He knew Santiago was dying. The pallor in his skin and the coldness of his hands told Martin as much. Though he heard Santiago's words, he dismissed them as the ramblings of a dying man. Distantly aware of Fernando beside him, Martin swallowed his petty grief and held Santiago in the only form of comfort he could offer.

Santiago smiled wistfully as the pain seemed to ease. He reached up and caressed Martin's cheek with a cold, trembling hand. His voice was barely more than a whisper. "*¡Mi nieto! Te quiero tanto, Como... Como tu madre y padre hizo.*"

Santiago's gaze remained fixed on Martin; the smile unfaltering. Martin caught the fragile hand as it drifted from his face and held it close. He did not know what else to say or do. From somewhere deep inside him, the words came, and he smiled with sad affection as he spoke. "*Sí, Abuelo. Ahora descansas.*"

Even as he spoke, Martin felt the strength leave the slender body as Santiago closed his eyes and his cheek fell against Martin's arm. The long fingers relaxed, and Santiago's last breath rattled from his breast as his soul departed.

Martin felt his throat close. Tears stung his eyes, and though he tried to hold them back, they washed down his scratched and dirt-smudged face.

A hand touched his shoulder. He looked up into Fernando's face. The man was pale with grief as he stared down at the vacant shell that had been his father. Martin remembered holding his mother's hand as she died and how he felt abandoned and broken by her death. Despite the shattered condition of his world, Fernando maintained his composure.

"Let's take him home," he said. "That is all we can do for him now." For a moment longer, he stayed there, then rose, bending beneath the low branches. "I will bring the horses."

He left Martin, still holding Santiago in his arms. Martin stared down into the death shrouded face and felt something tear part of his heart from his chest. In the first weeks, Martin knew him, Santiago had taken the place of a long absent mentor in Martin's life. That was why Martin called him *Abuelo*, and why, for the second time in his memory, Martin wept quietly for a loved one lost forever.

A soft breeze rustled through the live oak that cast a pleasant shadow over the open grave. At Fernando's solemn request, Martin joined him, Filipe, and Jinx in carrying the coffin from the parlor of the big house to the sprawling oak that shaded the family cemetery. It was a grim honor that Martin accepted numbly.

When they had laid Santiago in his earthen tomb, Martin stepped back behind the crowd out of respect for the family and friends who lived closest to the old man. Having known Santiago a brief time, he felt no right to mourn as deeply as they did, but the emptiness he felt held on despite his mind's rational thought.

The priest spoke, but Martin barely heard what he said, and didn't know if the priest spoke in Latin, Spanish, or English. He stared up into the great sweeping branches of the ancient oak and thought how Santiago must have chosen this place. In his last testament, he refused to be buried in the mission cemetery and, instead, wanted to be buried here among his ancestors in the shade of a tree planted by his great-grandfather. He smiled wistfully at the thought of Santiago, no longer tormented with the pains of a bad leg, stretched out in the grass enjoying the day as he had in life by appreciating the little things like a breath of wind or the warm sun.

Into these thoughts came Santiago's last moments, and what he chose for his last words. Santiago would never lie, but Martin's mind refused to trust the words. He had been too distracted, too determined to calm Santiago. What he remembered confused him, and searching for an answer left him feeling worn and tired. He tried instead to focus on the priest, but his attention drifted over the hills in the distance, noting the faded grass as it cured in the late summer heat. Before long, the rains would come, followed by winter. Another season would come and go in a relentless march of time that never heeded the coming and going of life among man or beast. It had been so when his mother died. It was so now that Santiago was gone. The same would happen when he breathed his last. What mattered was the time he had before the world moved on from him, and what he did to make things better for those left behind.

Martin filled his lungs and stared down at his hands, remembering Luis Alvarado's offer. He saw no other way to face the situation, but if he must die here, he would die bringing this feud to an end for the Terrazas. He knew the impossibility of a peaceful ending, and that Santiago would have frowned at the idea of killing his lifelong enemy, but maybe he would have accepted the idea knowing it meant the end of bloodshed.

Raising his head, Martin's gaze came to rest on Paco, standing with his head hung in grief and shame. He had told the story of what happened after returning from the mission with what help the padres could offer. Several of Alvarado's riders had caught them on their return from the mission, pulled him off the driver's seat, and spooked the team, sending the animals on a frightened run that ended in the wash. They had beaten Paco and left him on the roadside. After waking from unconsciousness, he had walked to the mission for help. Bruises covered his face. His left eye barely opened, and his jaw was still puffy from swelling. He walked stiffly from broken ribs. Judging by his injuries, he was lucky to be alive.

Kell must not have been with them; Martin thought wryly. Kell would have shot him for fun.

Regardless of who killed him, Santiago's death meant the end of waiting.

The priest blessed the grave, and those gathered around it crossed themselves, and all departed in a scattered sea of black.

A fresh wave of melancholy struck him at the sight of the grave, but Martin lingered and watched Bucho and Jinx cover the coffin.

Each hollow thud of soil against wood sent chills up Martin's back. The day his mother died came back to him. Her heart, her spirit, and her body had nothing left in them, worn down by grief for his lost father and the hardship of striving to provide for her child without a husband. His solace came in hoping she and his father were together now and at peace beyond the torments of this unforgiving world.

"Martin?"

He looked up into Filipe's grim face.

"Papa wants to speak with you when you have a moment."

He nodded, and Filipe turned away toward the house. His stride had lost its youthful confidence. It would return in time, Martin knew, but for a while, it would yield to sincere contemplation of mortality.

The men finished their work and left before Martin finally forced his body into motion and crossed the open field to the house. His boots sounded heavy in the still, empty hall as he followed it to the parlor, where he found Fernando standing by the cold fireplace. Martin didn't have to announce his presence.

"Come in, Martin," Fernando said without looking up.

Martin moved to the center of the room, hat in hand, and waited. For once, the silence did not wear on his nerves, and patience came easy.

"Have you nothing to say?"

"I'm sorry for your loss, *señor*," Martin said sincerely, and heard the pain in his own voice.

"That's not what I'm talking about." Fernando turned to face him. "I'm referring to my father's dying words."

Martin frowned. "I'm sorry. I didn't understand all what he said."

"Don't lie to me," Fernando snapped. "I know your Spanish is better than you claim. I heard what you said to him."

The reproach flowed past Martin. He held Fernando's gaze as he spoke with calm conviction.

"I thought it would calm him," Martin explained. "Wasn't 'Grandfather' an endearment for him? Even among those who were not his kin?"

Fernando nodded as anger flared in his eyes. "But he called you 'grandson.' *His* grandson!"

Rage flared in his eyes, and Fernando turned away, running his right hand through his hair as he paced between the edge of the rug and the fireplace. Martin wondered if Fernando's anger stemmed from jealousy. Santiago spent his last strength addressing Martin, with Fernando there at his side. Not Fernando, but Martin held him as he died because Santiago reached out to him. Martin bowed his head, knowing he had robbed Fernando of the opportunity to spend a final few moments with his father. Though he'd never known his own father, Martin knew how he would feel in Fernando's place.

"He spoke of it when you first came to us," Fernando continued calmly, though he continued pacing. "He *never* deviated from his belief. A dying man does not lie. He knows he will face judgment, and my father feared God more than any mortal."

"I don't doubt Señor Santiago spoke what he thought was true," Martin returned.

Fernando's pacing ceased. He faced Martin with eyebrows raised. "You don't believe you're his grandson?" he said in disbelief.

Martin swallowed and shook his head. He spoke softly. "I don't know what to believe anymore. Your own enemy claims me as *his* heir. How do I know I'm not just a pawn in y'all's game over land?"

Fernando blinked, but his anger lingered just beneath the surface.

"I have no doubt Alvarado tried to use you against us," he said. "Just as I have no doubt, my father was not mistaken."

Martin felt his blood heat with frustration. "How?" he challenged. "How do you know? I have no proof. Only my word and a story several years decayed in memory. It's only been in the last few weeks that I remembered my mother's language."

Fernando's expression softened. "When you came here, you had a picture."

Martin felt the daguerreotype's stiffness in his left breast pocket under his black vest, where he always carried it. Cold washed over him.

Fernando saw the flash of fear in his face, and his tone turned patient as he turned to the hall waving Martin along. "Come with me."

Obediently, Martin followed as Fernando led him down the hall to Santiago's room at the end. The heavy curtains, drawn across tall windows, admitted thin streams of light that failed to overcome the darkness.

"Years ago, when I was first married, Papa had a portrait painted of our family as it was then. Even after Mama died, he kept it in here." Fernando crossed the room and drew the curtains aside. Light spilled through, illuminating the room.

Above the mantle of the little fireplace, across from the bed, hung a portrait of a family smiling contentedly, except for one.

The old woman in the center scowled, her small, black eyes hard and piercing. Despite the artist's softening of her features, her visage sent a jolt of fear through Martin. A moment passed before he recognized the face of his nightmares as a child. That was the woman he remembered beating him with a heavy cane until he could no longer stand.

With a shake of his head, Martin pushed the memory away and forced his gaze over the other faces.

Then he saw her, the familiar face that the picture in his pocket had kept alive for him. She was younger, happier than he remembered, with autumnal copper in her hair and wild roses in her cheeks. His memory of her in life had faded to the colorless brown of the daguerreotype, which he withdrew from his pocket and stared at, comparing the two images to force his mind to believe his eyes.

Fernando put an arm around his shoulders.

"I should have known the night you brought Filipe home," he said in a hushed voice. "There is no mistaking your mother. You have her gentle heart and your father's fiery spirit. He would be proud of you."

Martin's throat tightened, but he forced the question.

"What kind of man was he?"

"Ambitious...strong. Bodie made things happen and rarely apologized for his mistakes. He came here to learn how to raise cattle. Now he has a ranch in the north country."

Tentative hope drove away Martin's sadness. "'Has?' You mean he's..."

"Alive? Yes, very much."

"But, Mother said Kiowas killed him when I was a child."

Fernando nodded. "I know, and that was what your grandmother led her to believe. By the time we learned the truth, you and your mother were lost to us," he seethed. "Mama hated Americans more than anything, and she hated everything. Your father and mother married against her wishes, and she lied to separate them. She knew the grief her actions brought about, and her efforts were truly intentional." He fell silent, haunted by this recollection. "When Papa found out what she had done, he threw her out of the house. She went back to Spain and died a few years later. We were all shocked by what she did, but we should have suspected after the way she treated you."

Again, Martin looked at the face of the scowling woman and felt that fear, remembering the pain from her beatings vividly. He couldn't remember what it was for. Now, he knew.

"You have no obligation to us here," Fernando went on. "You are free to go your way. To go to Oregon and find your family."

A thrill filled the emptiness of grief with hope. More than anything, Martin wanted to leave behind this place with its threats of bloodshed and death, but he knew he could not. As much as he now hoped for the safety and prosperity of the family he once believed gone, he wanted the same for the family he had found here. He couldn't leave with Alvarado's threats hanging over them.

"Santiago wanted to end this war between the Alvarados and Terrazas," Martin said when his throat relaxed enough to let him speak. He looked into Fernando's eyes with determination. "I intend to see that happen."

Fernando nodded slowly and turned away toward the dresser. There, on the simple linen drape, rested the brown paper package Jinx brought from the gun shop the day Santiago died. He picked up the package and held it out to Martin.

"You know Papa opposed fighting, but he believed that when a fight came, a man should be well prepared. He had these made for you."

Martin pocketed the picture and took the package. Through the wrapping, he could feel the hard, weighty contents. He laid the package on the bed, pulled the string, and unfolded the paper.

Inside, nestled together like two cottonmouth snakes in a den, was a pair of revolvers. Slowly, deliberately, he uncoiled the cartridge belt and drew one from a holster to examined it.

It was a Colt Peacemaker with a slightly shorter barrel and a cylinder adapted for .45 caliber brass cartridges. He pulled back the hammer to half cock and spun the cylinder. Its clicks blended in a *hiss* as unmistakable and unyielding as the sound of a rattlesnake's tail. The hammer moved smoothly and settled firmly as he thumbed it back to full cock. As he held it, the dark stained walnut grip felt natural against his palm and the weapon balanced perfectly, feeling more like an extension of his own body than an object apart.

"He knew you had no weapons of your own," Fernando said. "He also ordered this rifle to take matching cartridges."

Fernando flipped back the linen and exposed a Henry rifle. Its long, shining black barrel looked unlike those he remembered in the war. Instead of the brass plate, it had black steel. A forward stock fitted around the full-length magazine to protect the shooter's hand from the heat of repeated firing.

Martin returned the revolver to the holster and laid the rig on the bed before stepping to the dresser and picking up the rifle. It fitted naturally to his shoulder. As he sighted along the barrel at the corner of the room, the bead fell perfectly into the 'V' of the resting ladder sight.

Together, the three guns looked forged from the same blue steel and fitted with the same black-stained walnut. The holsters, cartridge belt, finely tooled with the swirls and puffs of an unfettered wind, were also black. Martin understood the symbolism.

"Instruments of death," he whispered.

"Or life, if used for the right purpose," Fernando prompted.

Martin nodded and hoped that when the time came, he would use these weapons with wisdom and justice and never bring shame to his family. As he thought of this, he felt a new sense of pride, but for so long, he had been without a name to honor that he feared his own inadequacy.

"*Señor...Tio*, would you promise me something?"

"Certainly."

His knuckles whitened as his grip tightened on the rifle. Once he spoke, Martin could not take back the words. His heart pained the way it had the first time he killed a man.

"Please don't tell anyone who I am until this business is over. That way...I won't disgrace you or the Terraza name."

Fernando frowned, studying Martin. "Why would you disgrace us?"

Martin shrugged. "In a fight, things happen." He shook his head, remembering what he had already done. "Things that make you cringe when you think back on them, and that others will judge you harshly for afterward. I only know how to fight to survive, and sometimes that means denying mercy."

Fernando remained silent a long while before nodding that he would keep the secret. Then he reached out and put his hand on Martin's shoulder. "I have faith you will honor the Terraza name in your own way and time."

A weak smile touched Martin's lips. He hoped Fernando was right.

The Breaking

The ranger seemed casual, almost lazy, but something lay beneath the surface that warned of his skill as a fighter.

Martin kept his distance from the man. If Fernando had not insisted on his presence when the ranger questioned Paco, he would have remained a stranger. Martin sensed this man was not one to like. A shadow hung over him that held the ranger distant from humanity despite his affable demeanor.

His name was Belden, and he showed no sign of malevolence as he paced the front room of the bunkhouse, but Paco still sat rigidly straight in his chair.

When he told it the first time, Paco spoke soberly, like a man disconnected from his thoughts. Now he told it with more emotion and gesticulation. When he finished, his hands settled into his lap, and he sat watching Belden pace around the bunkhouse table, hands behind his back and head bowed in thought.

From where Martin leaned against the wall, arms crossed, the sparse sunlight gave Paco's yellowing bruises a deeper shadow and lent him a ghoulish mask as he told the story again.

"Can you describe the men?" the ranger asked after a long silence. "What were they wearing? The horses they rode?"

Paco shrugged. "I don't really remember."

"Yes, you do," the ranger said firmly. "Tell me."

Paco seemed to think and again shook his head. "*Lo siento, señor.* I don't remember." He chuckled nervously.

Belden looked at Martin. His jaw worked, flexing in contemplation.

"Yes, you do," he said again in the same tone. "A man doesn't forget stuff like that unless he's witless, and you don't strike me as witless."

Paco stared down at the table in front of him and remained silent. Belden paced steadily toward Paco like a slow-moving rain cloud across the prairie.

"What, then, is keeping your tongue tied?" Belden asked, unclasping his hands and bracing against the table with his left hand. His right rested on the back of Paco's chair, effectively trapping Paco where he sat. "Is it fear?"

There was no change in Paco's expression or attitude. His head remained down, and his hands folded.

"Maybe they paid you to keep silent." Belden lowered his head as though to look into Paco's face.

Martin saw something in Paco's profile, a twitch of the muscles around his eyes. Three weeks ago, Martin saw Paco play a poker hand in which he won nearly two months' wages. That twitch passed over his face once when Bucho bet a month's wages. Either it had unnerved Paco or excited him. Martin was not sure which. Paco won that pot by a one card difference in a pair of kings and eights to Bucho's queens. Perhaps the tick now manifested because of Belden crowding him. His face twitched a second time as Belden began drumming his fingers.

Suddenly, Belden yanked Paco's chair back, slapped him hard on the chest, gripping his shirt and hauling him to his feet.

"I can make you talk," Belden warned. "You want to find out how?"

His action and his tone startled Martin, but Paco's expression seemed vacant, as though he were only a bystander to the violence. Then he looked into Belden's eyes as though his spirit returned to him.

"I will tell you," he said with a strange calm. He shrugged Belden's grip, picked up his chair, and sat back down.

Belden stood over him, watching as Paco ran his fingers through his mussed hair.

"There were five of them," Paco said. "Three *Tejanos* and two Americans. One of the Americans was a big man with a round face. He rode a buckskin. The other was lanky, like a fencepost. His face looked like the skin barely covered his skull."

Belden looked at Martin. "Sound familiar?"

Martin nodded. "Sounds like Kell and Rife. Neither was hired for their skill with horses or cattle."

The ranger nodded and turned back to Paco.

"One of the *Tejanos* was a little man, but broad-shouldered and rode a paint. The other two looked like brothers, the same coat and hat."

"Chico and the Morales Brothers," Martin spoke the names, then shook his head in unconscious disbelief. Chico's a good hand with horses and cattle. He favors a knife over a gun. The other two..." He grimaced. "Let's just say they'd sooner shoot a horse than ride it."

Belden's mouth was hard as he nodded. "I've heard of those two. Came up from Mexico a few years ago. Word has it; they cut their teeth riding with Comancheros."

Martin nodded once in understanding and glanced at Paco, who stared at him pleadingly, but Paco looked away when their gazes met.

"Can I go?" he said. "I don't know what else I can tell you, and I have work to do."

Belden considered his request and, at length, dismissed him.

Paco pushed up out of the chair and hurried outside without looking at either Martin or Belden. As he took down his hat from the peg beside the door, Martin caught the slightest tremble in the fingers. Martin did not blame him for being shaken.

"That's a queer thing to do," Belden commented. He crossed his arms and perched on the edge of the table with his left leg dangling. "That boy has lived on this ranch his whole life. Folks say he loved Santiago Terraza like his own kin, yet he fights to keep the identity of his killers to himself."

"Perhaps he was planning his own revenge," Martin suggested. He said it without thinking and regretted it afterward, fearing he betrayed his own desire to the lawman.

"Could be." Belden considered the thought a moment before shaking his head. Then his gaze turned to Martin and swept down to the revolvers.

Still unused to their weight, Martin felt uncomfortable under Belden's scrutiny, but he didn't squirm as Paco had.

"You know how to use those?" Belden asked at length.

Martin shrugged. "I handle them well enough."

Belden studied him, his gaze steady on Martin's face as he read the truth of Martin's words by the confidence in his voice. Knowing this, Martin studied the ranger in return. He was lean and raw-boned, tall as Martin, with hard blue eyes and brown hair bleaching to white. Belden's age remained a mystery, but Martin guessed his years had been hard ones. As Martin traced the lines of the man's face, a chill ran through him as though he glimpsed his own reflection.

After several heartbeats, Belden gave a nod.

"Maybe I'll find out for sure," he said. "I want you to ride with me tomorrow. You know the Alvarado boys better than anyone here."

Uneasiness filled Martin at the suggestion. He lowered his head to hide what might have shown in his face.

"Alvarado has put a price on my head," Martin told Belden. "If I ride with you, it may make things worse. Might even get you killed."

Belden listened in respectful silence, but his expression appeared unyielding.

"It's alright to be scared, kid," Belden smirked with a shake of his head. "God knows I scare easy enough. The truth, though, is that if you don't see this through, you'll be running from it the rest of your life. 'Course, a lot of folks say that who don't know the truth of it." His expression sobered. "So, here's the real truth. I don't trust Paco to be on our side. From what I've heard about that band Alvarado has working for him, I'd rather not turn my back on any of them. Mister Terraza tells me you were in the war and that you're trustworthy. Add to that your knowledge of Alvarado, and you're the best candidate for the job."

"Do you know why Alvarado wants me dead?"

"Yeah. And I also know that if you really intended to take him up on that offer, you wouldn't have let the Terrazas live this long."

Martin flexed his jaw, mildly irritated at the prospect of going back to Alvarado's place even for this purpose.

"Of course, you could go the other way."

Martin frowned and looked up at Belden in a silent question.

Sliding off the table, Belden paced toward him.

"This feud's been going on a long time. Hell! It's older than Texas. But things now are such that if one key person dies, this thing will end between these families."

The thought had occurred to Martin. Now that Belden suggested it, Martin wished he were back in Virginia. At least in the war, things were simpler and far clearer.

"Killing Alvarado would be murder," Belden continued. "But some would say that murder might be worth it. Might even save the lives of many on both sides."

Martin shook his head. "Santiago would not approve." He looked straight into Belden's eyes. "For that reason alone, I wouldn't do it."

Belden's eyes narrowed. "Perhaps, but things change. People change when they have the right reason to change."

He held Martin's gaze a moment longer as the meaning of his words sank in, then turned toward the door.

"We'll ride out at dawn tomorrow. Be ready."

"Yes, sir."

Taking his hat down from the peg, Belden stepped out the door and closed it behind him. The silence that fell over the bunkhouse left Martin's gut roiling as Belden's suggestion wandered around his mind. He could almost hear Santiago telling him that the choice of life and death rested solely in God's power. Should he assume such authority, Martin would incur the condemnation of both God and man.

"Times like this I wish I had your faith, *abuelo*," he whispered to himself. When the time came for action, he wouldn't have the luxury of thinking about what to do.

A roadrunner called from the brush as they rode through the dawn east toward Alvarado's ranch. Martin rode behind Paco and Belden. Like so many nights before a battle, he had neither slept nor eaten more than a few bites for supper or breakfast. As a result, he was in no mood for conversation.

Paco and Belden had exchanged few words since leaving the ranch, but tension lingered between them which further grated on Martin's nerves. The only thing keeping him from turning back was the promise of bringing Santiago's killers to justice.

With each step his horse took, Martin felt the weight of the revolvers on his hips and with it a resurgence of strength. There was something about a fight that never failed to make him feel alive. It was not an obsession with death or killing, but the movement of his body and the simplicity of bringing down an enemy, that appealed to him.

Having a last name still felt strange to Martin. He let his mind wander over the idea. He hoped thinking about it would make the idea settle and become real to him. Again, he wondered if he had been wise in asking Fernando to keep silent. He wanted so badly to call Fernando, Filipe, Maricruz, and Lucia his kin, but he wanted their safety with equal fervor. After today, they would know his true identity, and in a week or two, he would ride north to find his father and the home that he'd dreamed of since childhood.

The walls of Alvarado Rancho loomed into view over the lip of a high bluff. Belden drew up and sat surveying the place. Martin stopped beside him to watch the compound. He snatched a glance at Paco and felt a rise in irritation at the man's indifference.

"Not very busy this morning," Belden observed.

"Half the crew barely does anything before noon," Martin commented.

"Probably includes the ones we're looking for." Belden quirked his mouth in a wry smile. "Well, we've a job to do. Remember, let me do the talking. Just watch my back and don't start anything."

Martin nodded. "Yes, sir."

Belden heeled his horse forward at a casual walk. Martin glanced over at Paco, whose face looked pale and sick.

"The sooner we get this done, the sooner we can go home," Martin told him.

"I want no part of this," Paco grumbled.

Angered by Paco's persistent reluctance, Martin reached out and slapped a hand against the Tejano's chest, grasping his shirt and nearly pulling him out of the saddle.

"And I want no more of your whining! Santiago was like a grandfather to you, and you've fought us in every step of finding his killers. Why?"

Haze's flank twitched, reflecting Martin's agitation as he stared into Paco's face. His dark brown eyes narrowed into slits, and his mouth hardened as he stared at Martin. Then he slapped Martin's hand away, flashing his teeth in a snarl.

"I'll do my part," he snapped. "Just make sure you don't get me confused with the others and shoot me for the fun of it."

Martin scoffed humorlessly. "If only I were such a liar."

Paco's nostrils flared, and he kicked his bay hard, driving the gelding after Belden at a run.

Martin cursed silently. He had to keep his temper in check better than that, or he might get them all killed.

At his cue, Haze leaped into a run, and he soon caught up with the ranger and Paco. When they rode into the yard, Belden held the lead at a sedate walk. Martin and Paco flanked him loosely.

From all around the yard, the Tejanos looked up from their work in curiosity. A few frowned, but none stood ready to fight. Even so, Belden led directly to the main house, planting them squarely in the midst of Alvarado's supporters.

Absently, Martin wondered how Belden planned to get out the gate alive, even with him and Paco covering his back.

The kitchen door opened, and Martin saw Lolita freeze in the middle of throwing out a basin of water. Bruises marred her beautiful face. Her lower lip showed a barely healed split. Martin's blood boiled.

Their gazes met and held only a moment before she turned her face away and darted back inside, shutting the door.

Belden seemed as calm as the lazy stream running just behind the south wall as he led them up to the front porch of the main house. Before the ranger stepped down, Alvarado appeared at the door. His expression darkened when he saw Martin.

"What is the meaning of this?" he demanded of Belden as he cast his glare over the three of them.

Belden held up a hand in a gesture of peace. "Señor Alvarado, please, let me explain. I'm John Belden of the Texas Rangers. I'm investigating Santiago Terraza's murder."

Martin glanced back toward the chuck house at the sound of the door opening. If Belden heard it, he ignored it as Paco did. A line of Alvarado hands filed from the door. Rife and the Morales brothers were not among them. This worried Martin more than Armand and Kell combined.

Kell led them, swaggering as he always did, exuding malevolent confidence. He squinted proudly up at Martin, then reached into his pocket. Casually, he drew out a watch on a braided leather chain and twirled it. Martin's eye caught the flash of the familiar dove engraved in the lid, and he tried to swallow the anger rising in his breast. He moved Haze to the side and back, keeping Kell and the others in his line of sight.

"My men had nothing to do with that *bastardo*," Alvarado was saying. "Now, if you would kindly leave my hacienda…"

"Señor, I have no argument with you. I'm here as a lawman. Nothing more."

Paco snatched a glance at Kell. Seeing this, Kell turned his attention to Belden and wandered toward him.

Martin felt his skin crawl. Kell was the kind to intimidate a person to the point of breaking, and he was good at it.

Glancing over his shoulder, Martin spotted Chico holding back by the chuck house with Lolita tucked behind his shoulder. Red marks showed on his knuckles. When their eyes met, Chico pushed the girl back inside. Several feet beyond Chico, Martin spotted Armand coming from the barn, face bruised, and lips split, and knew what had happened between the three.

Armand's hand stroked the holster on his right hip. His left hand fingered the whip he always carried. He'd lost one fight and was primed to redeem himself with another.

Pivoting Haze with his right heel, he faced Armand and Chico. Belden would have to deal with Kell alone.

"Maybe we should just kill the three of you and leave it at that," Kell commented. "I know those two won't be missed." He gestured toward Martin and Paco with the watch clenched in his gnarled fist.

For the first time, Belden acknowledged the gunfighter.

"Shuck that gun," Belden told Kell so casually Martin doubted what he heard.

Taking Kell's cue Armand stepped out as his right hand jerked up, grasping his revolver.

Martin reacted, drawing his own gun and shouting, "Don't!"

Armand ignored him. The two fired at the same time, but Martin's aim was better, hitting Armand in the shoulder while Armand's bullet whined past his head.

Seeing the foreman reach for his shoulder, stagger and drop to the ground, Martin quickly turned to cover the others before they could slap leather.

They all stood gaping, frozen, shocked that the stable boy they had harassed, threatened, and beaten now had teeth. Even Chico, the only rider to show Martin kindness in this place, raised his hands to waist height, holding them wide.

"Shuck the gun belt, Chico," Martin called. "You're coming too."

Pale with resignation, Chico obeyed. Lolita ran to him. They whispered in Spanish as Chico tried to calm her. Martin risked a glance at Belden and Kell. The gunfighter looked genuinely shocked that the ranger held him at gunpoint.

Chico kissed Lolita as tears streamed down her face. He held her chin in his fingers, waiting until she nodded. Then he pulled away and stepped off the porch.

"I'll go without trouble," Chico told him, and Martin could hear a note of regret in his voice.

"I'm sorry," Martin said.

"So am I." He turned toward the others and ordered two boys to saddle horses for him and Kell. Chico smiled wryly up at Martin. "I'd rather not walk to my death."

Martin appreciated Chico's grim humor as he kept an eye on the men lining the front of the chuck house.

"I wish your boy over there hadn't started trouble," Belden said to Alvarado. "Might have to take him in too."

"You already have my two best protectors," Alvarado said. "Leave the man to die in peace."

"Your men certainly didn't do that for Terraza." Belden turned to Paco. "Go see if that man's still breathing."

Without a word, Paco turned his horse to pass between Martin and Belden. The woman who bent over Armand looked up at Paco as he rode beside the downed man. He spoke quietly, and she shook her head.

"He's dead, ranger," Paco reported.

Belden snorted. "You sure?"

"Yes, sir."

"Then get back over here." Belden jerked his head for emphasis. "Where are the horses for these two?"

"Coming." Martin nodded toward the barn. He kept his attention moving, keen for any sign of trouble. He glanced at Paco as he returned from checking Armand. Paco's gun remained holstered, but the fearful pallor from the morning had turned to a deep flush.

"You've come up in the world, whelp." Kell said, interrupting Martin's thoughts. He twirled the watch, wrapping the chain deftly around his fingers, so the watch slapped hard into his palm each time. His grin broadened when Martin met his gaze. Then he nodded at Haze. "Do all Terraza men ride horses like that, or are you just lucky?"

Belden glanced up at him, and Martin knew he, as well as Kell, waited for Martin to break, but Martin set his teeth and continued staring into Kell's cold, blue eyes. As he did, he watched the evil stirring there as the man's mind worked to find the hole in Martin's armor. He took a step forward, and Martin swung Haze's head, cutting the man off.

"No closer, Kell."

A chuckle bubbled up as though issuing from devil deep inside the man. Kell shook his head.

"You're afraid," he hissed. "Not of me anymore. No, you're afraid of yourself, 'cause you know you ain't that much different from me."

His words nearly broke Martin's composure, which was Kell's intention. Tenaciously, he held Kell's gaze, determined to hold it until Eternity swallowed both of them into hell, but the boys returned with the horses, and Martin was relieved when Kell looked away. Kell grinned as he pocketed the watch, Martin's watch, and climbed into the saddle.

Martin glanced down at Belden. "Get your horse. I have them covered."

Wordlessly, Belden gathered his reins and climbed aboard his dun. He nodded to Alvarado in a farewell gesture.

"*Gracias*, Señor Alvarado," he said. "Sorry to trouble you like this."

"This is nothing compared to the trouble you will face." Alvarado's attention focused on Martin. "Tell Fernando Terraza nothing changes. It is the same between us as it was between his father and me."

For a long moment, Martin held Alvarado's gaze. The old man's sapphire blue eyes sent a chill through him despite the blistering summer sun. He nodded once to acknowledge he would deliver the message.

Belden turned his horse and gestured for Paco to lead. Then Kell and Chico followed with Belden beside them. Martin brought up the rear, side-stepping the stallion to cover the remaining men standing on the chuck house porch.

Lolita stared pleadingly at Martin, but he could no longer offer her any comfort. Once they were clear of the gate, Martin continued several yards before turning Haze and letting him break into an easy lope.

As he neared the others, Kell glanced back, then leaned over and whispered something to Chico.

"Cut that," Belden ordered.

Kell ignored him, and Belden whacked him on the side of the head with his gun barrel. Kell yelped.

"What you do that for?" he screeched.

"You know why," Belden snapped. "Now, keep quiet, or I'll belt you again."

Kell's eyes narrowed. "Keep talking tough, lawman. Your time will come."

Belden stared at him. He cocked the revolver and leveled it with Kell's head. Kell's eyes widened, and his Adam's apple bobbed.

"Thought so." Belden stowed the revolver and fell back a step.

Martin stayed at the rear and watched the brush and hills beyond the trail. He thought of Rife and the Morales brothers and tried to think where they might be. Alvarado could have sent them out on the range days before, making them unaware of the arrests. Or they might have slipped out the back door of the chuck house. That was the difference between them and Kell. The big American enjoyed showing off. If he could make a fight, he would do so directly and loudly. Chico either thought himself innocent or, as he had at the ranch, admitted to doing wrong and would honorably face the consequences. Rife and the Morales brothers were different. Their way was quiet, deliberate, and rarely predictable.

Belden drew up and fell into step beside Martin.

"Think they'll ambush us?" he asked softly.

"There's a chance," Martin admitted, reassured that he wasn't the only one considering the possibility. "Got any plans if they do?" Martin asked.

"If I were you," Belden said and pointed to Kell and Chico, "I'd shoot those two. Then do my best to shoot the other three. I'm as much for justice as the next man, but you and I both know what will happen if any of them escape. They'll kill the three of us and wait to pick off the Terraza family one by one. Unless someone kills them first."

Martin admitted to himself he liked the idea of shooting Kell. The gunfighter lived to cause pain and suffering.

Chico, however, gave him pause. He remembered the man pleading for Kell not to shoot him in the wash, and it made Martin question whether the man took an active part in Santiago's death. Martin found himself weighing these two events against what he knew of the man.

Belden interrupted his thoughts.

"Keep sharp. If they hit us, it'll be in that juniper thicket two miles up. Best cover available before we reach Terraza range."

Martin nodded, and Belden kicked his horse into a trot to ride just behind and to the left of the prisoners. Martin remained vigilant, though his mind continued to wander. When he saw the rider coming up the road, his chest tightened until he recognized Fernando's palomino.

Fernando drew up and waited for them on the crest of the hill at the edge of the juniper forest. Momentary relief set in, as Martin surmised that if the ambushers waited for them, they would not have passed up the chance to kill Fernando. Then, on the heels of relief, came frustration at his uncle's disregard for his warning.

"Only two?" Fernando asked as they neared.

Belden nodded. "Ride with Martin. He'll tell you what happened."

"Like it's a secret," Kell chuckled. "We pulled one over on you, ranger, and you'll barely even know it."

Belden drew his gun to strike Kell again, but a shot rang out, and he stopped short.

Kell and Chico bolted for the brush. Martin drew and shot Kell in the back as he kicked Haze forward, trying to get between Fernando and the gunmen, but he had ridden too far back, and the second shot came almost on the heels of the first. Gunfire broke out from both sides of the road, and Fernando's palomino screamed in pain.

"*Tío!*" Martin cried as he fired blindly into the brush and spotted one of the Morales brothers behind a juniper. He charged the position, and as the man rose for a better shot, he killed him where he stood. Then he turned back to the other side of the road. But Rife fled, hot on Chico's heels as the other brother kneeled behind a sun-bleached log with his long gun.

A bullet burned Martin's left arm as Haze leaped over Belden's prone body, jarring his aim. His bullet missed and splintered the top of the log. The man worked the lever and fired another round. Haze reared, and Martin dove from the saddle, landing hard on the loose sand. He scrambled for cover behind a tree thirty feet from the man's position. As he switched guns, he snatched a glance toward the fallen palomino, hoping for a sign Fernando lived.

Dust whirled from behind the fallen horse as Fernando struggled to free his left leg from beneath the dead animal.

"Stay down, Fernando!" Martin ordered as the top of the man's head peeked from behind the horse's shoulder.

A laugh cut the sudden stillness, wet and weak as a shot made Martin jump. A last puff of dust rose from behind the palomino, like a soul rising to heaven as Fernando's hat rolled free.

Rage, hot as a smith's forge, shot through Martin. It rose in a scream to his lips and descended into his legs, driving him up and out from cover. He dropped into a roll as he flanked the log and fired two quick shots into the chest and head of the second Morales brother. Before the carcass hit the ground, Martin scrambled to his feet and vaulted the downed tree headed for where Kell had fallen.

Kell lay on his back, blood covering his chest and trickling from the corner of his mouth. He flashed a smile that displayed blood-stained stubs of rotten teeth and chuckled.

"Should have listened to him," Kell wheezed as Martin's pace slowed and he approached one leaden step at a time, fighting to keep his rage in check. "Alvarado makes good on his word."

Martin's whole body trembled as he stood over Kell. "And I make good on mine," Martin returned through clenched teeth.

Again, Kell laughed. "I'm dying, you son-of-a-bitch. What can you do to me now? No threat of death can reach me."

Martin's vision cleared. He saw Kell's horse and the lariat hanging from the saddle.

Without a word, he holstered his revolver and kicked the rifle out of Kell's reach. Then he retrieved the horse and took down the lariat.

Kell's eyes widened. "Wh... What are you doing?" Kell stuttered.

Martin shook out a small loop and could not deny the sense of satisfaction he felt at the blossoming horror on Kell's face.

"You always said hanging was the worst way to die...especially without a gallows." As he spoke, Martin his voice and his actions seemed distant, as though everything was part of a dream beyond his control. "Bleeding like you are, you'll pass out in a few minutes, but I have no intention of you dying so easily." He tossed the braided rope over a branch several feet over his head.

"Oh, God, no! Don't!"

Martin slipped the loop over his head and took up the slack. Kell gasped and struggled, trying to loosen the noose with bloodied hands as Martin wrapped the bitter end around the trunk of another tree and worked the rope, pulling down and taking up slack until Kell's feet left the ground.

The dying man writhed and kicked, twisting grotesquely as he dangled between earth and sky. Martin watched his struggles grow weaker until, at last, the body went limp and swayed like an inanimate marionette.

As the dead man swayed like a slow pendulum, Martin glared at the face in angry satisfaction. The throat was bloodied by the clawing hands; the eyes that an hour before mocked him no longer danced with that devilish spirit.

You know, you ain't that much different from me.

Remembering the words sobered Martin and cooled the violent lust that drove him into hanging the man. Kell had been right, and he had known it. Kell's proof was his death.

A cold, writhing sickness took Martin as he glared up at Kell's corpse. He remembered the watch and swallowed the rising bile. He stepped forward to retrieve the watch from the man's hip pocket. It was blood-smeared, but otherwise unmarked. Martin wiped it clean on his sleeve and slipped it into his vest pocket as he walked back to the road.

Kell's bullet had left no room for hope. He had shot Fernando through the head, killing him instantly. Martin stood beside the body, fists clenched, and a roar burst from the depths of his being. The rage and grief that filled it created an inhuman sound fit only for hell.

Heart of Darkness

The Terraza ranch buzzed restlessly as Martin neared the gate, but when he entered the yard, all fell silent. Men, women, and children stood watching him as he led the bay mare toward the main house burdened with Fernando's lifeless body. Martin rode with his gaze downcast, and when he looked up, he saw Filipe, Lucia, and Maricruz standing on the front porch. His throat tightened, silencing his voice. His gaze met Filipe's, but there was no warmth in his cousin's face, only virulent anger.

"How dare you come back here?" Filipe demanded.

Lucia, weeping into a handkerchief, timidly approached her husband's body. She buried her face in the blood-stained back of Fernando's coat.

"I've brought your father back," Martin said flatly.

"You killed him! Yet you have the arrogance to bring him here?" Filipe's fists balled at his sides. "Murderer!"

Angry shouts rose from the people gathered in the courtyard. Only this morning, these people had been his friends. Martin refused to look at them and fixed his attention on Filipe.

"Who told you I killed him?" Martin asked through the din.

"Paco. He told us everything."

Rage rose in Martin, but this time, grief and exhaustion kept it in check. He had not thought of Paco since before the ambush.

"Paco." He nodded. "You take the word of a coward? A snake who fled and left both your father and grandfather to be murdered?"

"Why should I take your word? Until two months ago, you were a stranger to us, and you have always been an enemy. I've known Paco since we were boys!"

Murmurs of assent barely drowned out the sound of Lucia's sobs. When last he looked into these faces, they wished him to go with God and prayed for St. Michael's protection over him. Now, they cried for his blood. Still, he loathed the thought of killing any of them to save his own life. Emotions warred within him as he looked deep into the face of the man he would always know as a cousin.

"I am no enemy to you," Martin said, his tone firm. "But I am a threat and always will be."

The crowd fell silent. Martin glanced around at their faces. He did not see Paco among them. He was grateful for that. Had Paco been there, he would have beaten the little coward to death. Instead, he found Jinx's weathered countenance and saw sadness and fear in the sun-bleached eyes.

"Santiago wanted this war to end. I will end it." He dropped the mare's reins and kneed Haze closer to the porch. He bent low and spoke for Felipe alone. "Bury your father, Filipe, and keep his name well."

Filipe held his gaze with a mix of grief, anger and understanding. He opened his mouth to speak, then swallowed the words. Finally, he said, "I hope none of my men ever catch you."

Martin straightened. "They won't."

With a slight pressure on the reins, Martin turned Haze toward the gate, deliberately turning his back to Filipe, placing himself at his cousin's mercy. The crowd parted, letting him go with only silent, stony stares to remember.

With no food, no bedroll, and no strength left to think, Martin turned up the road, not caring or knowing which way he went. He could return to Alvarado's ranch tonight and end it all, but Haze had as little strength left as Martin did. Both were grazed by bullets, and while Martin knew he could go on, he wanted to spare his horse the agony of running himself to death. With nowhere else to go, he turned toward the old mission and hoped the priest would grant him and his horse a night's rest.

From atop a knoll above the old mission, Jinx watched and waited. He had ridden many miles to make sure of his destination and then to hide his trail should anyone follow him. Now, as he sat cross-legged in the shadow of a juniper tree, he wondered how well Martin would receive him.

Two nights ago, he saw the look on Martin's face and failed to recall such a look of betrayal in fifty long years on this earth. He now waited for nightfall, hoping to catch Martin at ease with the two padres.

The sun touched the western horizon, and the shadows lengthened, then faded and vanished. Unfolding his long legs, Jinx rose, stretched, and limped to his horse. Rather than ride, he walked the mile downhill. A man on a horse posed a threat. A man leading a horse was an easy target.

The young padre met him at the heavy oak door.

"Has trouble befallen you, friend?" he called out as Jinx came near.

Jinx shook his head. "Not yet, padre." He squinted into the shadows beyond the doorway. "The man I'm looking for may cause me some, though."

The young padre's eyes narrowed at him. "Do you come as a friend or enemy?" he asked.

"A friend."

The young padre hesitated. A sound came from the shadows, and he cocked his head toward the door. Jinx felt his skin crawl as he recognized Martin's voice.

"You are a friend of Martin's?" the padre asked.

Jinx frowned. "I sure don't feel like one just now." He turned toward his saddle. "I just thought I'd bring his things to him. He'll be needing them before long." He started untying the bedroll when Martin's voice came from the shadows.

"Let him in, father."

Jinx looked past the padre, his skin still crawling. Though he knew the quietly friendly voice, something different sounded in its depths. Weariness made the words sound forced, effortful. Jinx continued untying the bedroll and took the extra saddlebags from in front of his saddle.

The young padre held out his hand toward the door. When Jinx stepped through, the figure lurking in the corner startled him.

All the youth and gentleness was gone from Martin's face. He looked pale, and his cheeks hollow. The torchlight above him cast deep shadows into his eyes and cheeks, giving him the appearance of Death incarnate.

"Hello, Jinx," he said roughly.

"Hello yourself," Jinx returned, trying to affect his old familiarity with the young man. "Reckon it's pointless to ask how you've been."

Martin held his gaze a moment before his attention shifted to the padre as he walked between them into the sanctuary. Then he fixed Jinx with a measuring stare.

"You took an awful risk bringing those few things," he said.

Jinx glanced down at the saddlebags and chuckled. "When a man lives in a saddle, these few things mean a lot."

For a moment, Martin studied him. His nod was slow and grim. "Thank you."

Jinx stepped forward and set the gear against the wall. As he straightened, he noticed Martin's torn sleeve and the bandage beneath.

"You get that the other day?" he asked.

"It's nothing," Martin replied.

Jinx shrugged. "Well, I guess I came for more than just returning your gear."

Martin tensed noticeably. "You come to collect a reward?"

"No. I came to warn you." Jinx folded his arms across his chest in a gesture of peace. "Filipe has sent for another ranger. After what Paco told him, those rangers will be hard pressed to see you hang."

"What did Paco tell them?"

"That you killed Belden and Fernando both. That he saw it, and that the men who killed Santiago said you told them how and when to do it." Jinx bit his lip. "He said you were in cahoots with Alvarado all along, since Alvarado claims you are his heir. Unfortunately, that's all anyone knows now."

For a long, grim moment, Jinx held Martin's gaze. The younger man was measuring him, gauging his friendship and trustworthiness. For all Martin knew now, he had no friends in this world.

"Do you believe it?" Martin asked.

Slowly, Jinx shook his head. He sighed.

"I know Santiago set a lot of store by you," he said. "I don't know the whole story, but I know his affection was not easily given. And I know what I've witnessed in my time. What I found yesterday morning on the trail to Alvarado's would have been proof alone."

Martin's jaw flexed, but he remained silent. The warning in his eyes was clear, but Jinx had no more patience for careful words.

"My suspicion," Jinx said neutrally, "is that son-of-a-bitch had it coming, and I doubt that anyone on his side would have done that to him."

Casually, Martin glanced toward the sanctuary. Jinx realized he stood on the threshold of a house of God. He removed his hat with a muttered apology to the Almighty while making a feeble attempt at signing himself. He stepped closer and whispered to Martin.

"I don't know what you're planning to do," he said. "But if it has anything to do with getting Fernando's and Santiago's killers, I want in."

Martin lowered his head, and the shadows in his face deepened.

"You don't want any part of what I'm going to do," he said grimly.

"I want to help you," Jinx pleaded.

Martin looked up sharply, his eyes catching the torchlight in sharp pinpoints that seemed to blaze in anger. Then, as quickly as it came, the expression ebbed, the fire faded, and Martin's gaze turned away.

"I'm wanted for three murders I did not commit," he whispered. "I reckon I'll give those rangers a reason to hunt me. You don't want any part of that. *I* don't want you to have any part of it."

A sharp sickness settled into Jinx's gut as he sensed malevolence in the young man he had helped give new life to. He remembered the boyish innocence that day at the corral when Haze chose him from the other cowhands. In the last two days, that innocence had disappeared, and in its place, a black serpent lay poised to strike. Despite his old man's cynicism, Jinx felt awkward and afraid.

"You're sure about that?" he questioned, toying with his hat.

Martin gazed into the sanctuary beyond the pews to the plain altar in front lit by dancing candlelight.

"My soul was lost long ago," Martin whispered. "I don't hope for redemption, but I'll die protecting my family."

Jinx felt a surge of hope. "Family?"

Martin shook his head. He regarded Jinx with the first friendly expression since the old cowhand's arrival. "Take care of them for me," he said and extended his hand. "And thank you, friend."

Observing the hesitant use of the word, Jinx took the offered hand, and forgave Martin for his lack of trust. Then he pulled on his hat and turned toward the door. Past the threshold, he paused and spoke over his shoulder.

"*Viaje con Dios, Martín.*"

Watching Jinx ride away, Martin felt his sadness deepen with the fading drum of hooves on the hardpan until the soft scrape of sandals on the stone floor distracted his thoughts.

"Perhaps you should have accepted his help, my son."

He glanced over his shoulder, thinking the old priest might be right, but rejected the idea as fueled by naivety. There was no sense in destroying another life. He picked up his bedroll and saddlebags and headed toward the back door. The old priest followed.

Outside in the little shed, Haze looked out over the rail that confined him in a stall. His ears pricked in Martin's direction. He fidgeted, ready for the trail. Martin dropped his gear next to the stall entrance and took the mecate bridle from where it lay across his saddle. He slipped it over Haze's head.

"Are you going to kill Alvarado?" the old priest asked.

Martin dropped the rail and led Haze from the narrow stall before he tied the rope to the snubbing post and reached for the saddle blanket to rub down Haze's back.

"I'll not preach to you about vengeance," the old priest continued as Martin worked. "I suspect you know that teaching well enough. Otherwise, you would not feel the guilt so heavy on your shoulders."

The declaration caught Martin off-guard like a bucket of cold water thrown in his face. His hands froze as he felt the burden of which the priest spoke.

But the priest stepped closer and told him in a confidential tone, "I joined your mother and father in marriage not long after I came to this mission. I also baptized you."

Martin blinked as his eyes stung. The image of his parents standing before the altar of this humble church rose in his mind and blocked out all other thought. He studied the priest, taking in the worn brown cassock and grayed hair. He knew the priest's words were true, but Alvarado's lies had shattered his trust, and his gut revolted against the logic his mind conjured.

"How do you know it was *my* mother and father? Not those of some long-dead child?" He bit out the words, unable to hide the anger he felt.

"Because I see their faces in yours."

Ice shot through Martin's heart as his desire to know and believe struggled against his fear of being wrong. Alvarado used him as a pawn. His mother, though her intentions were good, left him with no future. The family he trusted threw him out on the word of a lying coward. What, then, did this priest hope to gain?

"I remember them distinctly," the old priest said. "They loved each other so much. Your father was a gruff man when he first came here. Hard, even mean, but when he was with your mother, a gentler man, you never knew. Your mother glowed with pride the day they wed, and every day after that. She cared for your half-brothers with such devotion, one would think they were her own. That did not change when you were born. She possessed love enough for all three. And your brothers, they watched over you like the seraphim guarding the tabernacle. They loved to make you laugh. And you laughed much, even in church, when most other children cried."

From the priest's words rose a memory of two identical faces hovering over him, smiling, their words meaningless but unmistakable in their playful tones. For the moment that he remembered, Martin felt whole, happy, and no longer alone.

"Can you keep a secret, Father?" he asked.

The old priest smiled wryly. "I keep the secrets of all in my parish."

Martin met the old priest's gaze, and he nodded.

"I reckon I don't have to tell you after all," he muttered as he lifted the saddle onto Haze's back.

"Perhaps saying it will make it easier to believe," the old priest said. "Perhaps it will help make your path clear to you."

"I know my path, father," Martin replied, his voice deep with grim understanding.

"Is it the path you're choosing, or is it choosing you?"

Martin took a deep breath and held it as his hands tightened the cinch. When he came here two nights ago, the old priest had kept silent and granted him shelter while Haze rested. The priest asked nothing about the darkness Martin felt eating at his soul until now.

"If you kill Alvarado, you will destroy all the love your family had for you. You'll spend the rest of your days wandering creation, friendless and homeless until a bullet or a rope ends your life."

Weary with thinking over what he must do and what he wanted to do, Martin wanted nothing more than to shut his ears against the old priest's words, but part of him felt he needed to justify his resolution.

"That's true, father, but if I don't, how many more will die? Fifty? One hundred?" Martin glared at the old priest. "I know vengeance is a sin, and I don't care if it looks like that. As long as Alvarado lives, he will continue killing the Terrazas one by one, and I can't let that happen."

The old priest seemed crushed by Martin's words. He remained silent as Martin loaded his gear onto the saddle and checked his rifle. As Martin untied the *mecate*, he raised a hand, stopping Martin. "I pray God will forgive you."

Then the old priest turned and walked away, Leaving Martin with his heart in his throat. When the rectory door closed, Martin led Haze from under the awning and mounted up. From the gate, he turned east and traveled overland. Without a moon, traveling fast was impossible, but with no light, no one could follow him.

His left arm was still sore, but Haze's wound seemed little more than a scratch, and the big stallion's strength had returned within a day. If he chose his escape well, any pursuit would fall behind long before Martin reached the northern border. He had decided to end this fight while bringing Fernando's body back to his family, but his mind still wavered on who would die first. By the time the ghostly shadows of Alvarado's ranch emerged into view, he had decided.

Dismounting, he led Haze into an arroyo below the ranch and slipped up to the wall. He remembered a spot around the west wall where the hillside collapsed many years before. As he stood on the berm, he listened for signs of movement. Soft footfalls paced the fire step. He hoped it might be Rife or Chico.

He waited, and as the guard passed above him, Martin leaped, grasped the poles supporting the roof, and climbed over, landing lightly as a cat behind the guard. In a split second, he lunged and grabbed the guard around the neck, squeezing hard. The man struggled and, within moments, sagged to the walkway.

Pulling the body closer to the wall and tying the man's hands and feet, Martin searched the yard and listened for any sign that the struggle had alerted others. Then he looked down at the man's face. It was Diego, one of the stable boys, barely old enough to be called a man.

Martin stripped him of his poncho and turned him onto his stomach with his face toward the wall. Then he slipped the heavy cloth over his head and made his way toward the stairs.

Across from him, the other guard raised his rifle and waved. Martin gestured back, then descended to the yard, headed for the outhouse. Once within the shadows, he slipped around to the bunkhouse and climbed in through a back window.

His heart pounded with the fever of battle, and he stood for a moment in the room's darkness, listening to the sounds of sleeping men. One coughed and rolled in his blankets. Martin's heart stopped until the man's breathing deepened, and he once again slept soundly. With silent, stalking grace, Martin advanced into the darkness.

He found Rife's bunk first and found him cocooned in blankets, hiding his face. He eyed the gun belt hanging from the post, reached out and fingered the tooled leather and grips. Both butts faced the same direction, confirming it was Rife's. Despite that, he waited for another sign that this man was Rife.

It seemed an eternity before Rife moaned in his sleep and shifted onto his back. Starlight from the window fell across his face, and Martin had his proof.

Drawing his knife, Martin eased his knee onto the bedframe, hovering over the sleeping man. Like a striking rattler, he struck, pinning Rife to his bunk. His left hand covered the man's mouth in the same instant his knife pierced Rife's chest.

Rife's eyes shot open and stared wide at him, but Martin dragged the blade across and along the ribs, slicing open the heart beneath and prying downward to release the blood, letting it spill and soak into the blankets. Rife died quickly and silently.

Again, Martin waited and listened, but Rife's execution had gone unnoticed by his sleeping comrades. He rose, wiped his knife on the blankets, and moved to Chico's bunk.

It was empty. A cacophony of thoughts burst in his mind. Killing Chico was something he regretted having to do. He owed the man for keeping Kell from shooting him, but he also felt obligated to exact justice. He decided time was against finding Chico and slipped back out the window.

Glancing up at the sky, he estimated three hours before sunrise. That meant a three-hour head start once he ended Alvarado's life.

The other guard on the fire step didn't look down as Martin made his way from shadow to shadow to the kitchen door of the main house. Inky blackness greeted him within, and he groped his way through the faded smells of bread, spice, and ash to the main hall. There, like a beacon, he found a light burning in Alvarado's room.

For a moment, he stood outside the door, listening. Then he lifted the latch and stepped inside.

The old man looked up from his book, his expression eternally stern.

"*I told you I did not want to be disturbed*," he said in Spanish.

Martin kept his head down as he closed the door and turned to face Alvarado.

"*One of the men is dead, señor*," he replied, affecting Diego's voice as best he could remember it. "*Killed in his bed.*"

Alvarado slammed his book shut and pushed up from his chair. "*By whom?*" he demanded.

"*We don't know, señor*," Martin replied, reaching for the knife at the small of his back. "*Perhaps one of Terraza's men.*"

Alvarado scoffed. "*Man? There's not a man among them.*" He turned his back to Martin, facing his wardrobe. "*Which was killed?*"

"*Rife, señor.*" Martin waited for the man to look down from the mirror. Then, in two quick strides, he closed the distance between them and pressed the knife to Alvarado's back.

"Tell me, señor," he whispered. "What possessed you to claim me as your grandson?"

There was no fear in Alvarado's face as he lifted his gaze to the reflection and looked squarely into Martin's eyes. He smiled.

"So you've come, finally," he said as though addressing an old friend. "I've waited for a long time."

Martin frowned. "Answer me, old man. Why did you claim me as your kin?"

Alvarado chuckled. "Two years ago, a gypsy caravan traveled through here. The old woman read my fortune. She told me death would come from the seed of my enemy, *un muchacho con ojos oros*. When you appeared on my doorstep that night, I knew you for Maitea's son. I thought I could save my life by turning you against your own. When I couldn't, I tried to break your spirit."

"By killing Santiago?"

"*Si*." Alvarado hung his head. "I've known you would come for a while, *La Muerte*. I am ready for you."

Martin drew a deep breath and sighed, sensing the irony. "You know what your one mistake was, Alvarado?"

The old man merely shifted his gaze.

"I hadn't considered killing you before Santiago's death. When they killed Fernando, that was the final cast. You've brought this on your own head."

"And what comes from this, *Muerto*, will be on yours. My family will never stop hunting you."

As Martin met his reflected gaze, he felt cold, calculated rage turn his veins to ice. Alvarado was the last of his lineage. His ranch would fall into ruin; its workers scatter to the wind. What family was left to avenge his death?

A knock sounded on the door, and a woman's voice called softly.

Alvarado filled his lungs to shout, but Martin clamped a hand over his mouth and brought the knife around. He cut deep into the old man's throat.

Alvarado reached up, grasping the wound out of reflex and catching Martin's sleeve, but as his body sagged back onto the bed, he sneered in a final expression of triumph.

The knock sounded again, more urgently. Martin pulled free of the dying man, but before he reached the window, the door opened, and Lolita stepped through with a thin robe pulled tightly around her body. Her eyes widened in fear at the sight of him. When she saw Alvarado lying across the bed, heart stilled, and eyes fixed and glazed in death, relief relaxed her features.

"Go," she whispered calmly. "I'll not tell them."

"They'll think you did it," Martin replied.

"I'll tell them I found him like this. That I don't know who killed him." Her words came in a hurried rush. She skirted the bed and put her hands on his arms. "If they catch you, they will kill you. Now go!"

He glanced at the dead man, and a thought occurred to him. "Where's Chico?"

"Gone. He came back for his things two days ago and left. Said he wanted no part of this anymore."

"And left you at the mercy of these *pendejos*?"

"It's what he had to do," she snapped back. "I've lived this way since before womanhood, and it will never change."

Martin's stomach twisted at the realization of what she meant. Any man could have his pleasure with her, and she was powerless to stop them. It did not differ from slavery, and he hated himself for not understanding sooner or doing something about it.

"Come with me," he begged. "You deserve better than what's here for you."

"Like what? Starvation?" Anger flared in her turbulent eyes, but her voice remained soft, even gentle. "I have a roof over my head, clothes on my back, and food in my belly. As long as I have that, I have enough."

"No one should live like this, Lolita," Martin growled back. "No woman should have to trade her virtue to fulfill her needs."

Her eyes narrowed at him. "And you would risk getting caught to save me? *Baboso*, go before I kill you myself." She shoved him toward the window. "Go!"

He hesitated, trying to think of another way to convince her. She looked around and found Alvarado's revolver resting on the bedside table. She picked it up and leveled it with Martin's heart. Her hand did not waver, but tears sparkled in her eyes.

"Go, or I'll spare you the slow death they'll give you."

Her hand was steady, but her voice wasn't. Somewhere along the way, she'd grown fond of him, he could see that in her eyes, but there was no dissuading her when she made up her mind.

Without a word, Martin slipped the poncho over his head and turned to the window. He looked out first to be sure the coast was clear, then swung a leg over the sill. He looked back at Lolita one last time.

"Where did Chico go?"

"*Norte*. Now go!"

He tried to think of something to say in farewell, but Lolita cocked the hammer, and he knew his time was up. He lowered himself to the ground.

Blinded from the lamplight, he crouched beside the wall and waited for his eyes to adjust. When he could see the fire step, he gauged the distance to the ladder and decided the front gate would be an easier way of escape.

Keeping low, he moved toward the front of the house and slipped into the shadow of the old oak tree. The man on the fire step had turned and paced toward the front gate. Martin's heart pounded as he realized he was plainly visible to anyone who looked out from the bunkhouse. Then, the guard paused, gazing down at the outhouse, puzzlement barely visible in the starlight. Martin had wasted too much time, and before long, they would discover Diego.

Martin forced himself to calm and wait for the right moment. If he spooked and ran too soon, the guard would certainly see him.

The man paused above the latrine and called to Diego. Above the thudding of Martin's heart, he heard the muffled cry from Diego on the far side of the house.

The guard looked up and started walking around the wall. Once he passed out of sight behind the house, Martin would run for the gate.

Then, a thought occurred to him. If he left the gate open, it would lead them directly to his trail.

Praying the guard wouldn't look his way, he climbed the gate, using the strapping and bar for holds. He heard the first shout from the guard as he vaulted over the top and dropped to the ground on the other side. The second shout covered the sound of his landing. He broke into a run for the arroyo and slipped into the mesquite, circling back to his horse.

Escape from Texas

The following days stretched together. He rested little and then only for Haze's benefit. More than once, he was thankful for the stallion's enduring strength and did all he could to preserve it.

He watched the south for the ever-present dust cloud, signaling the location of his pursuers, and tried to think how to outsmart them. He hoped to strike the Brazos River and find it shallow enough to wade along it far enough south they would lose his tracks. Perhaps he could follow it as far as Austin and gather supplies. The heavy wagon traffic would obliterate his trail, but if someone had wired the capitol with his description, they'd recognize him, and a new posse would give chase.

It was the second day by the time he reached the water and felt relief to see it ran low for the season. Haze took to the water willingly, and both man and horse welcomed the cool moisture. Martin kept Haze close to the bank, where the water sloshed at the stallion's knees. For a half-hour Martin rode before dismounting and leading Haze on. The current was with them and made the going easy, but he wanted to spare the horse the extra burden of his weight. Nearly an hour and a half after entering the water, they climbed up the bank and pressed east.

By sundown, the dust cloud had disappeared, easing his conscious fear of capture, but nightmares still filled his sleep that night, and he woke up unable to breathe from the tightness in his throat.

He had little hope of finding the man while on the run. Still, the desire to do so lingered with him.

After a week of hard riding, he spotted a settlement and paused in the cover of a sprawling live oak tree to consider the wisdom of riding in. The jerked beef Jinx provided had run out two days before, and he couldn't risk hunting or loose time snaring. As he crouched and studied the settlement, he glanced over at his horse.

Haze looked worn and dozed with his head down. Martin worried he pushed the animal too hard. By now, his name and likeness could hang on every lawman's poster board. If anyone recognized him, he ran the risks of running Haze to death. Still, he needed food, ammunition, and, if possible, a place to hide. Part of him wanted to know how avidly the law wanted him, or if only Alvarado's men pursued him.

Stretching his hand toward the western horizon, he determined two hours remained before sundown. Three would bring the full dark he needed to disguise Haze's mottled brown coat. Folks might write him off as another drifter, but if any reports described the brown stallion, questions would arise.

Martin cursed. He didn't like the situation but saw no other option. He settled down against the tree trunk and waited.

As he watched the sun drift down the western sky, his mind wandered. He thought of his cousins and aunt in their grief. Could things have been different if they knew who he was? Martin shook his head dismissively. He still would have killed Alvarado and disgraced them. This way, he brought all the trouble onto himself, leaving them free to live out their lives.

Shame washed over him as he thought of his mother. Only after committing murder did he think of her and how she would have wept for his immortal soul. She had been a peaceful woman despite her fiery temper. Martin could imagine the look on her face, but her words and the sound of her voice eluded him long ago.

From his breast pocket, he drew out the old portrait and studied the faces of his parents. His mother, with a subdued smile, sat in a high-backed cushioned chair, a veil cascading down over her hair from a crown-like comb, her head held high and regal. Beside her, his father stared sternly, back straight and proud, his left arm draped across the back of the chair with a protective air. He seemed a giant compared to her, broad-shouldered and light-haired. His features betrayed Nordic heritage.

Martin knew he more closely resembled his mother in his slight build and Spanish features, but somehow, he had inherited his father's fighting spirit and a subtle resemblance in his build. Would his father recognize him when they met? Did he dare confess his identity? If Texas wanted him for murder, he could not tell them who he was without putting his family in danger. Lifting his gaze to the north, he thought of the miles that lay between him and Oregon. He thought of the chilly nights, dry days, and the dangers he would face every time he entered a settlement like the one below and realized he likely would never meet his family. His throat tightened with grief, and he again shook his head. Too many nights without sleep had eroded his immunity to emotion.

Tucking the tintype away in its place, he removed his hat and slouched deeper against the tree. He dozed and opened his eyes to find the sky black save for a thin glow in the west. People still moved around the settlement. He mounted up and rode into town at a sedate walk, avoiding the brighter lit parts of the street.

Hope slipped away as he passed one dark store after another. Then, he spotted a general store with the light still glowing, and his hope rebounded.

Glancing back, the way he had come and on up the street to be sure no one noticed him, he turned Haze up an adjacent alley and left him ground hitched. Walking casually, he stepped up to the porch and tried the door. It swung open easily, but the ring of the bell startled him.

The proprietor glanced up from a ledger he had laid out on the counter.

"We're closed, mister. You'll have to come back in the morning."

"Sorry," Martin said. "I was just hoping to pick up some hardtack and dried beef."

"And that can't wait 'til morning?" The man's tone betrayed a short temper, and Martin's hand drifted closer to his gun.

"I'm riding out tonight," he said casually. "I haven't got much, but I'll pay what I can for the inconvenience."

The proprietor's eyes narrowed as he studied Martin. He had a round face, button eyes, and wore a twill vest that strained around his middle. As Martin watched, understanding came over the man like a cascade starting at his brow and descending to his lips.

"*El Muerto*," he whispered, horror running as an undercurrent through his tone.

Martin raised a hand as though he could soothe the man's fear. "I mean you no harm, mister. I just need some food and grain for my horse."

"You mean to kill me for it?" Panic was rapidly taking over the man, and Martin scrambled for a plan to deal with him.

"No," he replied flatly. "I'll pay you in script, and I'll take your word you won't go running to the law right away."

Understanding seemed to break through the man's growing panic. Then his expression lit with an idea, and all common sense fled him.

"What if I refuse?" he asked with a tone of challenge.

Drawing a deep breath, Martin gritted his teeth. "You don't want to know."

He knew it was a bluff, but in a brief lapse of awareness, he believed his own threat. What mattered was that the proprietor believed him. The man's gaze darted to the window over Martin's shoulder, making his skin crawl. He moved deeper into the store.

"When does the law make rounds?" Martin asked.

"Just about this time of night," the proprietor replied. "You should leave before Marshall Rawlins gets here. He'll shoot you dead without question."

Martin had to hand it to the man. He knew how to take advantage of an opportunity, but because of the context, Martin called the bluff.

"Thanks for the advice," he said, "but I'll take my chances. Now, if you don't mind, I'd like a pound each of jerked beef and hard-tack and four pounds of grain.

Frustration flashed over the proprietor's face. His mouth hardened. "I don't negotiate with thieves and murderers."

With a sigh, Martin drew his left-hand revolver with casual irritation. "In that case, mister, I'll ask you to show me where you keep your rope."

"You're going to tie me up?"

"Yes, sir, and I'll club you over the head, if need be, but I'd rather not. I'd rather you go home to your family tonight, eat at your own table and sleep in your own bed, but if you keep up this mule-headed bullshit, you'll be spending the night here or at the doc's with a split skull. It's your choice."

The man frowned in puzzlement. "You really don't want to hurt me?"

Martin shook his head once, and the proprietor nodded.

"Alright," he said, sliding off his stool. "I'll get what you ask."

Martin holstered the revolver and followed the man toward the back of the store. Dividing his attention between the windows and the proprietor taxed his senses, but anxiety kept him alert. His nerves tightened more at the proprietor's silence as he collected the items and brought them to the front counter.

"That will be two dollars, four bits," he said.

Reaching into his pocket, Martin froze at the sound of footfalls on the porch. He did not dare look up in case the passerby recognized him. Silently, he prayed the steps would continue down the boardwalk, but they stopped at the door, the knob clicked, and the bell rang.

"Evenin', Clare," a man's voice greeted. "Thought you closed an hour ago."

"Rawlins," the proprietor returned, meeting Martin's gaze with mild triumph. "Was just helping this gentleman with a few supplies."

"Oh?" The marshal leaned an elbow against the countertop. "Couldn't wait 'til morning?"

"No. He's in a bit of a hurry to head north."

As casually as Martin could, he counted out the payment from the coin in his pocket and collected the sack of groceries with his left hand.

The marshal rolled his head back in contemplation as he studied Martin's face. "Where you coming from, son?"

Martin fixed the proprietor with a questioning look, expecting him to answer that question as well, but the man kept silent, and Martin did not offer an answer.

The marshal's eyes narrowed. He straightened.

"You know, I noticed that dappled brown horse in the alley. He yours, son?" As he spoke, he straightened, letting his hand rest against the revolver on his hip.

"Don't do it, Marshal," Martin said coolly, despite the shock of fear piercing his heart.

"You think you can take me?" the marshal challenged with a smirk.

For the first time, Martin met the man's gaze. He knew the lawman didn't stand a chance against him in an even draw. His gun was ill-kept, riding high and loose on his hip. Excitement coursed through the lawman just beneath the surface of his flushed face. He may wear a badge, but it was clear he could not live up to the purpose of his office.

"Before I kill you," Martin said casually, as if it were a polite conversation between them, "mind telling me how much I'm worth to you?"

The lawman blinked. "There's a combined reward of four thousand dollars on your head, Martin."

Martin nodded and scoffed. "I guess killing you will add another five hundred." The corner of his mouth lifted in a sad smile. "All over two and a half dollars in grain and foodstuff. Should've just let myself starve."

"You could come along quiet, make it easy on both of us."

An alarm went off in Martin's head, too late to head off the fight. The proprietor, moving slow and careful, had reached his hidden revolver and drawn it, thumbing back the hammer as he brought it into line.

On reflex, Martin swept up his right-hand revolver and shot the man without thought, then turned as the lawman's gun barked. In less than a heartbeat, two men died in the cramped little store, their blood running over the worn floorboards. Before realization could sink in, Martin darted for the back door. Shouts came from the main street as he snatched the trailing rein and swung aboard Haze. He spurred Haze into a dead run into the back alley, but he did not dare stay there for fear that he'd get trapped.

With a turn as sharp as any cutting horse, Haze darted back toward the main street, leaping a pile of trash and cutting close to a suited man who yelped in surprise.

"Shoot him!" someone shouted.

Martin held tight to the saddle as Haze wove through the crowd of people, then flattened against the stallion's neck as the horse stretched into a full run, as though he knew the urgency of their situation.

The buildings blurred past and fell away. The quarter moon had yet to rise, but the road stretched like a white ribbon through the grass under a starry sky. Martin let Haze run all-out for a half mile before drawing up and sliding to the ground. He pulled a piece of jerky from the bag and tucked the rest with the hardtack into the right saddlebag. Then, he let Haze have a portion of the grain, all the while listening and watching for pursuit. He lingered just long enough to finish half the beef strip and let Haze have a breather. Then he put the grain away and climbed into the saddle, but as he lifted his right leg to clear the bedroll, a sharp pain knocked the breath from him. The world spun, and he clung to the saddle horn until it passed. He looked down at his side and saw a dark patch glisten on his shirt.

He growled in frustration and pressed a hand to the wound as he kneed Haze forward.

They walked for several miles while Martin tried to stop the bleeding. He wasn't sure, but he believed it was only a deep graze. At first, the pain cleared his head, then wore him down to the point he lost track of the miles. He did not remember the moon rising or giving Haze his head. He dropped into a deep sleep and woke up to the sharp scent of sage and the first rays of dawn lighting the east. Haze stood beside him, quietly grazing on the sparse grass.

For a long moment, Martin fought to remember where he was, and as the memories returned, he questioned if it had all been a dream until he tried to sit up. He looked at his horse apologetically.

"I got us in a real mess, didn't I?"

Teeth grinding on the dry vegetation, Haze glanced over his shoulder, ears perked forward.

"I'll take that as agreement," Martin groaned. He collected his hat and staggered to his feet. He took down his canteen and shook it. His heart sank to find it was barely a quarter full. Lifting his shirt, he inspected the wound. It needed cleaning, but Haze needed the water to keep going. Taking a swig, Martin offered the majority to the horse, then wet his neckerchief. Gritting his teeth, he cleared away the worst of the blood and found it was indeed a deep graze that had bled badly, but it showed no signs of infection, though it was stiff and sore.

Still holding his side, he put up the canteen and climbed back into the saddle. Clouds had moved in during the night, bringing a chilling wind. He pulled on his oilskin slicker and watched for rain as he rode. It appeared as a veil descending from the low clouds to the west, obscuring the gently rolling hills as it drew closer.

It broke over them around noon after he refilled his canteen, and both he and Haze had drunk their fill at a shallow, muddy stream. All morning, he had watched the north but only saw an occasional puff of dust. He had not thought to head south, but now it worked out.

As the clouds broke, he turned Haze upstream and hunched his shoulders against the driving west wind. A half-mile later, he left the water in a downpour that washed out their tracks and headed north again.

The late summer rains swelled the creeks and rivers by the second day. After nearly drowning on the third crossing, Martin decided just to follow the banks of the next river he came to. Haze had grown worn and weary and walked with his proud head hung. To spare him, Martin walked with the horse heeled beside him like a dog, using him for balance when the mud got deep.

It was late the fourth day when he came to the bridge. The river running beneath it, gorged on rain, washed out the banks. The girders and planks creaked and groaned as they crossed. Haze hesitated. When Martin coaxed him forward, Haze threw up his head and tried to pull back.

"Easy, Hazy Boy," Martin soothed as he stroked the stallion's muzzle. "We have to cross this river. The sooner we get out of Texas, the better. They can't chase us forever."

Haze calmed. Whether it was Martin's encouragement or the stallion's faith in him, Martin did not care. Haze followed him calmly onto the bridge. As they neared the far side, Haze's ears perked, and above the rush of water, Martin could hear a soft cry.

"Hello?" he called out.

The cry intensified, with words unintelligible above the roar. Martin followed the sound down along the bank. There, clinging to a willow root, was a little girl.

The bank was steep and slick. Though Martin could reach her, he risked falling in with her.

Taking his lariat, he tied off the lasso end to the saddle horn.

"Stand, Haze."

The stallion's ears perked toward him as he descended the bank, but he stood firm.

The girl wept loudly. Her little hands were blue with cold as they clung to the root.

"I'm coming!" Martin shouted. "Hold on!"

He spoke too soon as the bank gave out under him, and he slid into the water upstream of her. She screamed as he collided with the root and knocked her loose, but he dove forward, and his hand shot out to grasp her arm in a precarious grip. In desperation, she lunged toward him and gripped the sleeve of his oilskin with both hands. He pulled her closer, wrapping his arm around her body.

"Pull, Haze!"

Steadily, one step at a time, Haze backed away, pulling them to safety. Roots and rocks dug into his ribs and back as Haze dragged them onto solid ground. At Martin's command, Haze stopped and stood.

For a long moment, Martin lay in the matted grass and let the rain fall on his face while he caught his breath. The girl pressed her face to his shoulder and hiccupped with sobs.

"It's alright now," Martin told the girl as he sat up. He untangled his stiffened fingers from the lariat and brushed the dark hair back from the girl's face. "Are you hurt?"

She shook her head and sniffed. "I was just trying to get out of the rain. I tried to crawl under the bridge and fell in. Papa's going to be so angry!"

"He would have been angrier if you had drowned in that river. Come on. Let's get you home."

Still crying, but determined, she got to her feet and followed Martin to where Haze stood, looking curiously at her.

"What's your name?" he asked as he untied his bedroll to wrap her in it.

"M...Mary," she stammered through chattering teeth.

"Alright, Mary, we can't make a fire, but we'll wrap you up nice against the rain." He unfolded the blanket and draped it around her shoulders, then the tarpaulin shell to help keep out the rain. As he did, Martin glanced toward the bridge and saw the bank had collapsed up against the footings. Before long, it would no longer hold the weight of a horse.

"Where's your home, Mary?"

She pointed to the far side of the bridge. "That way. About a mile past the fork."

He felt his shoulders sag. He could not leave the girl here alone, but if he took her home, he risked getting trapped on the south side of the river with a posse on his trail.

"How far from here?" he asked.

"A mile."

He heaved a quiet sigh and rose from the mud. "Let's get you home. No point in staying out here any longer."

Martin put away the lariat and lifted the girl into the saddle. "Hold tight now. If we fall in, you hang on to Haze here. He could swim through a hurricane." He smiled, hoping to cheer the girl. She gripped the saddle horn with both hands.

He led Haze across the bridge, ears keen to the creak of wood as it moaned beneath their feet. He prayed it would hold, and in a mixed blessing, it did, until they reached the far bank. As Martin climbed into the saddle behind the girl, he heard the hiss and splash of the bank sloughing out from beneath the footings, followed by the groaning and popping of lumber as the bridge twisted and broke, scattering lumber into the floodwaters.

The girl shivered. "Pa's going to be angry," she said through chattering teeth.

"Ain't much he can do about it." He unbuttoned the slicker and wrapped it around her, hoping his body heat would help keep the girl warm, but the chill was working into his own bones. "Which way?"

The girl only pointed, and Martin turned Haze down the road. Gradually, the girl stopped shivering. She curled up against Martin and fell asleep. As they rode, he could feel a fresh trickle of water down his collar. He reached up to adjust his hat and realized it was gone, probably lost when he fell in the water, a minor loss compared to the revolvers, but his jaw tightened in frustration. He made note to take off his guns next time he attempted such a rescue. Had he not tied himself to Haze, the extra weight would have dragged him down into the water. The hat had been a gift from Filipe. Things being as they were, it was probably just as well.

An hour after leaving the river, they rode into the yard of a well-kept little homestead. The animals were out of sight, penned up against the rain. As they neared the house, Martin noticed the sagging heads of wild roses lining the front.

The front door flew open, and a tall man in a slicker and hat hurried out to meet them. Behind him, a woman stood backlit by the flickering light of a fire. She called the girl's name.

The girl woke at the sound of her mother's voice. Mary looked up, and when she saw the man, she stretched her arms out to him. "Pa!"

Martin lowered Mary into her father's embrace.

"My God! Where have you been?"

"I fell in the river," Mary explained. "He saved me."

The man eyed Martin. A fresh chill ran up Martin's spine as he nodded in greeting. Rather than risk trouble, he decided it was best to leave soon.

"Thank you, stranger," the man said genuinely, though his expression remained guarded.

"It's no trouble."

"He fell in too, Pa," Mary added. "His horse pulled us out. Can they stay with us for the night? Please?"

Despite his daughter's plea, the man seemed no more welcoming.

"That's alright, Mary," Martin said to soothe the girl. "I still have a long way to go. You folks take care now." He reined Haze back down the road, and the man returned to the house carrying Mary.

"Please don't go," the woman called from the porch.

Martin turned back as the scent of wood smoke from the chimney reached him. His stomach twisted with hunger and a shiver of cold ran through him. Against his better judgement, he desired warmth and human contact.

The woman spoke to the man as he set Mary on the top step beside her. Martin couldn't hear their conversation above the rain. The man shook his head, but the woman spoke again, and the man obligingly walked back out into the rain.

"Why don't you come inside and warm up, stranger," the man said. Though his words were friendly, his tone held an edge.

"I don't want to be any trouble," Martin replied.

The man shook his head. "Looks like you and your horse could use a rest, and no one should be out in this storm. I was just fixing to go after Mary when you rode in."

Martin turned his gaze back to the road, torn between fear and want. Until then, he had not realized how weary he was. Haze needed rest more than he did, but something in the man's manner scared Martin.

"Please," the man continued. "A warm fire and a hot meal are the least we can do for saving our daughter."

Again, Martin's stomach twisted, and he realized he had eaten nothing in two days. He relented, but as he stepped down, the man took the reins and offered his hand.

"Bill Knolls," he said. "My wife is Anna, and you've met Mary, our daughter."

Martin took the extended hand, but his mind failed to create a name for himself.

Bill noticed this but took it in stride. "I'll take care of your horse for you." His way was firm, and Martin decided not to fight him. Instead, he took his rifle and the soaked bedroll.

"If you can spare some grain for him, I'd be grateful."

Bill smiled. "I'm sure I can."

Martin returned the smile with a tired nod and walked up to the house. The door stood ajar, but when he stuck his head inside, the front room was empty.

"Be out in a minute," the woman's voice called from the back room. "Just make yourself at home."

Feeling awkward, Martin retreated outside to shake what water he could from the slicker, then hung it on a peg beside the door. From where he stood, he could hear Mary telling her mother what had happened in great detail. If not for the weariness, Martin might have smiled at the excitement in the girl's voice, but he only glanced around the room, taking in the gun rack beside the china hutch, the little table, the rug between it and the open fireplace, and the two chairs flanking it. Beside the hearth, a wooden horse stood in a miniature corral, gazing stoically upon the swirling, braided pattern of the rug.

Pulling a barely dry rag from his saddlebags, he sat on the stone hearth and began wiping down his guns. The cartridge belt was soaked as was the ammunition, but before he could recover his saddlebags and the dry cartridges inside it, Anna bustled out from the back room. She had blonde hair and a bright, kind face that invited Martin to trust her, but he kept his gaze averted.

"Mary insisted on going to school today," she said as she busied herself in the kitchen. "I tried to keep her home, but she refused to listen. I feel terrible."

The sound of Bill's footsteps on the porch drew Martin's attention. He put away his left-hand revolver and drew a deep, calming breath.

Anna turned an innocent smile on him and filled a cup of coffee. "Thank God for you. Mary told me you were nearly caught in the flood trying to save her."

Martin said nothing as the door opened, and Bill stepped in, slicker in hand. He hung the coat and hat beside Martin's worn slicker, and as Bill turned toward the fire, the flash of a silver badge stopped Martin's heart. Resting a little heavier against the hearthstone, Martin kept his gaze on Bill. The knife in its leather sheath dug into his back. It did not reassure him, but it took the edge off his sense of vulnerability.

"That horse of yours has put down some miles," Bill said conversationally. "Where were you heading?"

"Wherever I could get," Martin replied in an attempt at friendliness.

Bill scoffed. "Not many places you can get in this rain. I'm surprised the bridge to Wichita Falls hasn't fallen in."

"It did, just after your daughter and I crossed it."

Bill cursed quietly. "Guess I won't be going to town for a while."

Martin turned his gaze to the flames and hoped the heat would hide the sudden chill running through his veins.

"Where's Mary?" Bill asked his wife.

"In bed," Anna replied as she brought an iron pot and hung it over the fireplace. "I'll bring her some food. You're welcome to sleep here by the fire, stranger."

It took Martin a moment to realize she was talking to him. "Thank you, ma'am."

She smiled and returned to the sideboard to mix biscuit dough.

Bill sank into the rocking chair facing Martin, sighed, and dug a pipe from his pocket. Out of the corner of his eye, Martin saw his attention catch and linger on the revolvers. He feigned ignorance of the man's curiosity, picked up a splint, and toyed with it while Bill packed his pipe.

"What's your line of work?" Bill asked, again attempting conversation.

"Cattle," Martin responded after a moment.

"Drover?"

Martin nodded. "When I can," he lied. "Between jobs at the moment."

Bill nodded. "Seems that's the way to make money since they started driving north and east. They pay well?"

"Well enough for my needs," Martin replied.

Again, Bill nodded and openly eyed the guns, but he said nothing as he put the pipe between his teeth. Martin touched the splint to a burning log, lighting it. He held it while Bill puffed the tobacco into flame.

Martin studied Bill as he lit the pipe. He was not far into his twenties, a deputy sheriff, according to his badge, but his expression and manner were wise. Martin relaxed a fraction when he realized this man was smart enough to not try something in front of his wife or daughter. That also meant he was smart enough to gain an edge before tipping his hand, and in his current state of exhaustion, Martin stood no chance against him in a battle of wits.

If Bill was aware of Martin's scrutiny, he gave no sign and thanked Martin genially as he sat back in his chair.

Anna nestled the biscuits in a Dutch oven and settled it into the coals. As she straightened, she noticed the bloodstain on Martin's side.

"You're hurt!"

Martin held up a hand to ward off any offer of help. "It's alright, ma'am. I just tangled with a branch a few days ago." The lie came easily, but like a doctor feeling a pulse, Bill watched him while quietly puffing on the pipe.

"Even a little cut can turn septic," Anna warned. "You're sure you wouldn't like to clean it."

"Maybe later." He offered her a smile. "I'd really rather just sit here and dry out, ma'am."

"I have some antiseptic. I'll get it."

As she stepped between them, headed for the back bedroom, Bill caught Martin's attention and held it. The deputy was smart. He knew the truth, and in his gaze lay a quiet warning. Anna left the door open, and both men could hear her speaking to Mary. In a gesture of good faith, Martin folded his hands in plain sight and kept them there. Bill pursed his lips and nodded in satisfaction.

"Here you are." Anna handed him a bottle and a scrap of cloth. She went to the water bucket and ladled water into the basin she pulled from the cabinet then set it on the hearth beside him with a cloth. Then she kneeled beside him and started lifting his shirt.

"Please, ma'am." He caught her hand and held it firmly but gently. He did not want her to see the wound, lest she could tell the difference between a bullet graze and the lash of a branch.

"No need to be modest," Anna countered. "I've tended enough of 'Bill's wounds in his life."

Bill scoffed and puffed his pipe. Reluctantly, Martin relaxed his grip. She showed no sign of unease at Martin's resistance to her care and no shock at the sight of the wound.

"It's a little red," she commented as her fingertips traced the swelling. "But it's healing." She dipped the cloth and pressed it over the wound. Martin tensed, but made no sound.

"You said you tangled with a branch?" Bill asked. Martin nodded.

"Was trying to find a place to hole up out of the rain," he lied. "My horse ran me into a tree."

Bill hummed thoughtfully at this information. Martin wondered how good a judge of horses Bill was.

Anna finished with the water and soaked the cloth with antiseptic.

"This will sting," she warned.

Martin nodded he understood, but he wasn't prepared for the explosion of fire on his side. By the time the burning eased, he could barely keep his eyes open.

"Hold this," Anna instructed, putting his right hand on the cloth. Then she straightened to check the stew. "We'll wrap it. Keep the infection out."

"That carbolic probably just burned out whatever infection he might've had," Bill teased his wife. "She's a great believer in it."

Martin scoffed and nodded agreement, then realized there was no trace of a joke in Bill's expression. Bill betrayed no fear or even genuine concern. Anna sensed it, for she fixed her husband with a gently imploring gaze.

"Take off the badge, Bill. This man is our guest."

Bill looked up at her, then over at Martin, weighing his choices. With Anna standing so close, Martin doubted Bill would try to shoot him. He could easily reach out and pull the woman to him as a shield. Perhaps Bill thought the same thing, for he reached up with his left hand, unpinned the badge, and laid it beside him on the table.

Anna nodded approval. "Good." Then she went back to the bedroom and returned with a rolled bandage.

"Lift your shirt," she instructed.

Martin obeyed, and she wrapped the bandage just above the line of his belt.

"There. Feel better?"

Martin smiled gratefully. "Yes, ma'am. Thank you."

"Thank you for saving our daughter."

Her words and the touch of her hand on his arm were the first signs of friendship he had experienced since the day before Fernando died. Even at the mission, the padres held him at a distance, whether out of respect or pious devotion.

Anna must have understood how deeply her kindness affected him. After gazing into his eyes for a moment, she patted his arm, straightened, and started serving the stew. Even Bill's expression had softened some.

Anna considerately set the place nearest the fire but sitting there required Martin to place his back toward Bill for the duration of his meal. Deciding to take the chance and show faith he did not feel, Martin moved to the table and ate.

Anna disappeared into the bedroom to feed the girl, taking with her the calm Martin felt until then. He ate slowly despite the ravenous hunger. He finished the stew and two biscuits in uneasy silence.

Finished with his pipe, Bill pushed up out of the rocking chair with a groan and tapped the ashes from the bowl into the fireplace. He returned to the chair, making enough noise that Martin easily followed his movement.

"Would you like more?" Anna asked when she returned from the bedroom with a tray balanced against her hip.

Martin shook his head. "Thank you, but no."

"You look like you've been a while without a hot meal."

He feigned a shy smile. "Believe my stomach's shrunk from it, ma'am. But thank you. It was very good."

She glanced at her husband but gave no acknowledgment to his sulking mood.

"I believe I'll clean up and turn in," Anna said as she cleared the table. "Help yourself to more coffee. Bill, will you give me a hand?"

Bill's gaze locked with Martin's, questioning rather than warning this time. The man did not want his wife to worry, and Martin did not blame him, but standing at the washtub would put his back squarely to Martin. Deliberately, Martin cradled his coffee in both hands and nodded toward the woman, a silent promise he would not harm either of them.

Bill tapped his holster deliberately as he rose slowly and turned to the washtub.

Martin filled his cup again from the pot beside the fire and watched the windows. A chill ran up his spine. His whole body felt heavy with exhaustion and craved the warmth of the hearth.

"Reckon I'll sit close to the fire," he said, giving Bill ample warning of his intentions. Then he sank down beside the fire again. He knew it was unwise to sleep in such company, but it crept upon him and pounced soon after he sat down. He woke a few minutes later to a light tap on his arm. Fortunately, he came to quickly enough to realize Mary stood next to him before reaching for a weapon.

"You startled me, little one."

Without pretense, the girl wrapped her arms around his neck in a powerful hug. After overcoming this second surprise, he hugged her back, keenly aware of the moisture in his clothes soaking into the girl's thin cotton nightdress.

"Thank you," she said in his ear and kissed his cheek.

He patted her back and swallowed the lump forming in his throat. "You're welcome." In that moment, he did not care if he died tonight. This family was complete, whole, and loving. Only that mattered to him. "Careful, you'll get all wet again."

"Don't you have any other clothes?"

Martin coughed and glanced up to see Bill and Anna watching them. With a weak smile, he shook his head.

"I'll be alright. Now you go on to bed."

But the girl remained. "Will you be here in the morning?"

"Maybe," he told her. "If I'm not, you be a good girl and mind your ma and pa."

Mary nodded that she would and trotted away. She stopped at the door and waved. "Good night, mister."

Martin waved back, and the girl disappeared into the back room. He settled back and picked up his coffee as the sound of clanking dishes resumed. Glancing up, he caught Bill watching him, but the deputy's expression had lost its edge.

A log settled in the fireplace sending embers up the chimney. Martin watched the flames dance across its surface. He wondered briefly if his brothers had children. By his reckoning, his brothers would be near thirty. Likely, they were settled with families, probably on their own homesteads.

The clank of a dish on the floor made him jump. His right hand dropped to the revolver as his gaze shot to Bill, but the deputy, stone-faced, bent and picked up the plate. Martin's heart continued pounding long after the plate was washed and put up. Consciously, he relaxed his muscles, but tension lingered. He tilted his head back and tried to remember what he was thinking before the noise, but his mind refused to grasp it.

Finished with the dishes, Anna took the basin to the door and tossed the water onto the saturated ground. Bill put up the last plate and hung up the towel.

"Will you be staying up a while, dear?" Anna asked Bill, who nodded.

"I'll be up a little while yet." He hooked his thumbs in his belt and gazed down at Martin. Martin caught a frown of displeasure on Anna's face.

"Bill, you'll see to our guest's comfort?" Anna took Bill's arm. Martin averted his eyes, giving them what privacy he could without leaving the hearth.

"I will, Anna." Bill bent and kissed her cheek. "I'll be in before long."

"Don't be too long." She passed the rocking chair and paused. "I'll never be able to thank you enough, stranger."

A flood of thoughts froze his tongue. How could he express the value of her courtesy? Instead, he smiled his quiet smile, bowed his head briefly, and said, "Have a good night, ma'am."

"And you have the same." Her smile seemed so warm, so gentle, Martin remembered his mother and how much he missed such kindness.

She retreated to the other room at the back. The latch clicked into place, and Martin was alone with Bill. In Anna's absence, a chill settled over the room again. Martin felt more than saw Bill's hand inching close to his gun.

"Don't," Martin whispered loud enough for the man to hear without his voice carrying through the closed door. "Don't make me kill you here, where your family will have to know and remember."

"Strange sentiment coming from a murderer," Bill whispered back.

Martin smirked and nodded. "I suppose it is." He lifted his gaze to the man. "Only I have some sense of family. Being an orphan, I know the pain of loss."

"Did you think of that when you killed that ranger and your employer? Terraza had a family."

A fresh pain knifed his heart. Martin lowered his gaze. "Care to hear my side of things?"

Bill scoffed dismissively. "You'll just claim you're innocent, that someone else killed those men."

"No. I killed my share, but that's not what I'm referring to."

Bill frowned in confusion. His right hand lingered against the leather of his holster. As Martin sat with his arms crossed, he was at a disadvantage, but he wouldn't give up easily.

"You've got a good thing here, Bill," Martin continued. "Before a couple of weeks ago, it was something I'd thought I'd lost forever. Then I found hope of having it again, a family to love and care for, and to rely on when I needed them. Then things happened, I had to make a choice, and that choice cost me that dream." He fixed Bill with a look that was equal parts plea and warning. "Take my advice, Bill; don't take the chance of losing what you have here."

Bill's expression softened as he considered this. He glanced toward the bedroom door, and the rigidity left his spine. He swallowed.

"I can't just let you walk out of here," he said.

"Yes, you can," Martin responded. "I'll not spend the night, and when Anna and Mary wake in the morning, they'll wonder if it really happened. In a few days, they'll forget I was ever here."

The deputy seemed unconvinced. His right hand twitched, and Martin relaxed his arms, readying himself to fight.

"Don't risk it," Martin pleaded. "You may kill me, but I'll kill you too. Which do you think Anna would rather have? The reward money? Or the husband she loves? Warm, alive, and loving like you are toward her and your little girl?"

"You're just trying to talk yourself out of this," Bill countered.

"Am I?" Martin let the challenge hang before going on. "That store clerk had the same choice...so did the marshal. They chose to take me, and they both died, and I walked away with a single scratch, nothing more. You're one man. Think you'll be luckier than those two combined?"

In the dancing firelight, the color drained from Bill's face. His shoulders sagged.

"Alright," he said finally. "I owe you for saving my daughter, but I'll not let you stay in my house."

Martin nodded. Moving deliberately, he rose from the hearth, his clothes still damp, but that was a small price to pay for leaving this family as he had found it and better than it would have been without him. He pulled on his slicker and collected his rifle and saddlebags.

"Martin."

He stopped at the sound of his name and waited for Bill to speak.

"Thank you for talking me out of it."

Weary from long miles and worn by these last few moments, Martin could only offer a nod before stepping out the door and heading to the barn.

The rain had eased. He saddled up and headed north again, pausing to look back at the homestead where the firelight still glowed in the front windows. What happened there paled compared to his sins of days before, but this small victory buoyed his spirits, and he rode on, thankful for his good horse, the smell of wet earth and sage, and even for the chill that lingered well after dawn.

The Red River roared like a hungry cougar bringing down game. Martin stopped at the edge of the water and climbed down from the saddle to stretch. His sides ached from the nagging cough that had started the day before. He kneeled as Haze cropped grass and considered which direction to follow. Thought had become an effort almost beyond him with every additional day adding its share of fatigue. Many times in the war, he and those he fought beside had marched and fought on willpower alone, but rest had always been in sight. Now, he pushed on, unsure if any rest would come without death. To focus, he closed his eyes and bowed his head, willing the tension in his body to ease.

The morning was cool and still. A light breeze swept through the prairie of North Texas. Fall was coming, and for a moment, he laughed at himself for heading north into a cold, white winter, but he could not stay in Texas. New Mexico and Arizona held only vast loneliness and reaching them required several more weeks in a land that wanted his execution. North was the only direction left open to him, whatever he found.

Through the stillness, Martin heard a distant shot. He opened his eyes and listened. Another shot came from upstream. He climbed into the saddle and turned Haze east along the line of willows at a quick lope.

In a small hollow, a man lay dead. Two others hunkered, one behind a wagon, the other behind a log. Martin stumbled into the open , right into a crossfire.

The man behind the wagon shot at him. Martin veered Haze to the left, drew, and fired back on reflex. A second round from the other man whistled past his head so close his ear tingled. Haze whirled as the man in black and white prisoner's stripes, stood up for a better shot. Martin killed him with two rounds in the chest.

The prisoner wilted like a dropped rope, and Martin turned back to the wagon where the man behind it now lay still. He circled around and drew up staring down at a Texas Ranger badge pinned to blood-stained gray vest. Martin felt sick at his poor luck, and knew things held no promise of improving. He slid off his horse and crouched beside the dying man, taking the revolver from his limp fingers.

Struggling to breathe, the man looked up at him. Blood foamed at his mouth, and the wound in his chest sucked and hissed.

"I didn't know," Martin muttered in apology.

"You're not...one of the gang?"

Martin shook his head.

The ranger laughed, and the laugh grew into a racking cough that ended in a wheeze. Martin went to his horse for a canteen. He kneeled beside the ranger and offered water. The ranger pushed it away.

"Don't waste it," he said. "Did you get him?"

Martin nodded. "He's over yonder."

"Least that's done." The ranger's eyes wandered to the distance. "Which way you headed?"

"North."

The ranger grunted understanding. "Goin' by Amarillo?"

"Maybe."

With his right shoulder shattered, the ranger reached awkwardly across his body and dug a watch from his hip pocket. He handed it to Martin and unpinned his badge.

"Take that," he said of the watch, "to the teacher, Miss Leighton. Tell her I love her." He gulped air before going on. "Take my badge, and Carl's..." He nodded toward the dead man a few feet away. "...to the ranger captain up there. Tell him what happened."

Martin stared down at the badge smeared with blood, the sickness thickening. He looked back at the ranger. His mouth now gaped in a futile effort for breath. He reached out with his remaining good hand and, gripping Martin's arm, pulled himself up. Martin held him there, the bloody fingers digging deep through the cloth until the ranger's eyes lost focus and his muscles relaxed. Martin eased him back against the wagon wheel, but the hand remained clamped on his arm, frozen in a vice-like death grip. The back of his throat tingled. He tried to pry the fingers loose, but they refused to bend. The dead ranger's eyes still stared at him, and Martin had the sudden irrational image of the dead man dragging him down into Hell.

Steeling himself against the nightmarish image, Martin drew his knife. He sliced the wrist, spilling blood not yet clotted. The fingers relaxed, and Martin worked his sleeve free. The hand dropped with a light thud to the sandy ground, and Martin scrambled away to a willow thicket. There, the sickness overcame him. On hands and knees, he heaved, his stomach empty. When the convulsions stopped, he remained there, trembling. Ironically, he felt thankful he consumed only water that morning, having no food to eat. Martin sat back on his heels and filled his lungs with cool morning air before a fit of coughing seized him. When it ended, he sat hunched and winded. His side and head ached worse now, and he deserved it.

Glancing over his shoulder at the scene, he wished it had only been a dream. Texas once meant hope for him. Now it only meant sleepless nights and dreams with the faces of dead men constantly reminding him of the trail he followed to his own grave.

On shaking legs, he walked down to the river and rinsed his mouth. Then, with dutiful weariness, he searched the wagon for a shovel. Finding none, he took a plate from beside the fire.

It took a day and a half to dig two graves in the muddy earth. The rangers he buried first, covering them with what stones he could find. Deciding the dead men would not need what they left behind. He searched their pockets before he covered them, finding ten dollars and a letter between the two corpses. Too exhausted to dig a third grave, Martin left the prisoner where he fell, despite the ongoing noise of scavengers gorging themselves on his flesh. According to the letter, the prisoner was a member of the Jackson gang that raided along the border of the Indian Nations, and Martin did not care to further abuse his skinned and bloodied hands to give a man like that a proper burial.

As the ranger asked, Martin took the watch and the two badges and rode north, keeping to low ground where possible. He camped without fire despite the constant chill and worsening cough. With what lay behind him in that hollow, he had reason to worry. Jackson's gang roamed this country, and if they found the prisoner's body, the trail Martin left would not be hard to follow. Once or twice, it occurred to him he was being a fool. What did it matter that the ranger's sweetheart knew he was dead or not? But the thought of leaving it undone left a worse sense of dread in the pit of his stomach than the threat of being caught. He realized the senselessness of this but ignored his better judgement.

The small town of Amarillo looked as thin as Martin felt when he rode down the main street six days after the rangers' deaths. He paused near the general store and gazed down the street at what looked like a church a few hundred yards outside of town. Framed by the setting sun, it looked no different from any other building.

"Help you, stranger?"

Martin glanced over into the eyes of a man with a sheriff's badge and nearly laughed at his luck for finding lawmen without trying. He quickly buried the wry humor. "I'm looking for Miss Leighton. Would she be over to the school?"

The lawman shook his head. "T'day's Saturday. No school held today."

"Where might I find her?"

"Why are you asking?" The man settled his left hand on his hip. His right palm rested against a holster with a well-worn gun nestled inside. His finger tapped the leather lightly in absent thought, an unconscious habit. Wearily, Martin took it as a warning.

"It's my concern, sheriff," he said calmly. "I don't intend trouble."

The lawman studied him, his expression filled with doubt. Martin gave him time to think in still silence. He had no intention of letting the sun set with him in this town, but rushing a lawman could get him pushed out sooner or settled in the jail at the far end of town. Finally, the lawman nodded toward the schoolhouse.

"Down at the end of the street," the sheriff said. "You'll find a little wagon trail leads out behind that church to a rooming house. Ask for her there."

"Thank you." Martin nodded to him and walked Haze to the end of town. All the while, he was aware of the stares from the people on the boardwalks and the street. They were the typical stares such settlers gave drifters, or so he tried to convince himself. Still, he felt a small measure of relief once he was out of sight down the little wagon trail.

The shack barely qualified as a rooming house, one story with a lean-to added on one side for a small extra room. Martin worried he took the wrong turn or misunderstood the sheriff's directions. He stopped at the gate, unsure whether to proceed or turn back, when a woman stepped out on the porch. She ran her hands down her apron, and Martin realized it was near the evening meal.

"Come on in," she called. "The gate's not locked."

Martin nodded and leaned down to unlatch the gate. He rode through and closed the gate without dismounting. The little farmyard was clean with chickens and a handful of goats loitering near the haystack. Haze pricked his ears at the goats and snorted a warning. Martin slapped the stallion's neck with a sharp, "No," and Haze continued forward, but his left ear pivoted toward the little herd.

Martin turned his attention to the woman on the porch. She was thin faced with a harsh expression. Her hair was drawn back in a tight bun. Martin wondered if her expression came from the hairstyle.

"Have we met before?" the woman asked, cocking her head as Martin neared the porch.

"No, ma'am."

She set her hands on her hips. "If you've come for food, I haven't anything for drifters."

Her tone cut deep, but Martin forced down his reaction.

"Thanks, ma'am, but I've come on another matter." A shiver ran up Martin's back. Despite it, his skin felt hot. "I'm looking for Miss Leighton. Might you be her?"

"No, I'm Missus Reardon. I own this place. Alice Leighton is my tenant."

"May I speak with her?" He barely finished before he noticed her standing in the doorway. She stepped forward. Young, pale, and dark-haired, Martin saw why the ranger had taken to her.

"What is it?" She read the grim lines on Martin's face.

Martin dismounted and climbed the steps to stand before her. He reached for his hat and remembered he had none.

"Miss Leighton…" His throat tightened, cutting off his words. He looked down at the porch boards as he reached inside his vest pocket. "I've brought you this," he said finally, holding out the watch.

She took it and stared at the plain gold case. When she opened the lid, her beautiful lips parted, and her cheeks blanched.

"It's Dillon's." Her hand went to her mouth as tears welled in her eyes. "How did you get this?"

"Your man was killed in a shootout," Martin explained. "I was with him when he died. He asked me to bring you this and tell you he loved you."

Her eyes flared. "Is that all?"

"Yes, ma'am."

She glared at him, then turned away sharply and disappeared inside, slamming the door behind her.

Martin didn't move. Words of apology burned inside him, but their sheer inadequacy kept him silent.

"Is that all you came for?"

He glanced at Missus Reardon. Her face, ashen by nature, had taken on a deeper frown.

"Yes, ma'am." He descended the steps, depriving her of the opportunity to order him off her property. When he reached Haze, he turned back. "Could you tell me where I might find the captain of rangers?"

"Captain Neil lives at the jail. He dislikes his own cooking. So, if you don't find him there, he'll be at a cafe."

"Much obliged, ma'am." Martin climbed back into the saddle.

Missus Reardon stood on the porch, arms crossed, watching him leave.

Martin exited the gate and turned Haze back down the trail to Amarillo, glad to be done with the task. He had hoped that by telling Miss Leighton, some of the weight would be lifted from his shoulders. Instead, it rested heavier. Telling her had been easy. Seeing her grief hurt him as much as the ranger's death.

Little daylight remained when he walked his horse back through town to the jail. With no one there, he led Haze down to the livery for water, then returned and waited for the lawman in a chair left beside the door, where he fell asleep. He awoke to find two men with badges staring down at him.

"You're looking to get charged with loitering, son," the white-haired one said with more mirth than malice.

Martin ran his hands over his face. The sun was gone. He'd have to wait nearly an hour for the moon or ride slowly if he rode at all. He looked back up at the lawmen and recognized the sheriff.

"We tolerate little from saddle tramps in this town," the sheriff said. Silent warning exuded from his posture and tone.

Ignoring the comment, Martin looked at the other wearing the ranger's star. "Would you be Captain Neil?"

The man nodded.

"If I could speak to you for a few minutes, I'll be on my way."

"Certainly. Come inside." He unlocked the door and stepped into the darkness, where he struck a match and lit a lamp on the desk. The sheriff followed, but Martin held back at the doorway.

Neil checked the pot on the cold stove. He glanced back at Martin and waved him inside. "Come on in. We don't bite unless you're a lawbreaker. Sorry, I don't have any coffee to offer."

"That's alright." Martin took a step across the threshold, eyeing the walls. How long since he stood inside a building? Too long, and the quarters felt too close.

"Could I get you some water?" Neil asked.

"No. Thank you."

The captain turned a mildly puzzled look on him. "In a hurry?"

Martin stupidly shot the man a look, and his blood chilled. "Not particularly," he replied in his best attempt at a casual tone.

"Well, if you don't mind, I would like a cup of coffee while we parlay. Have a seat."

Reaching up for his hat, Martin self-consciously ran his fingers through his shaggy hair. He sat down in the chair at the front of the desk facing the door. Inwardly he cursed himself for tipping his hand. He had to slow down and let them have some control. If he kept calm, casual, he would walk away from this and go on with his life.

Leaving his hat on the rack beside the door, Neil went out back with the coffee pot and returned with it filled with water. He added grounds to the percolator and stoked the fire in the little stove.

The sheriff took a seat behind the other desk in the corner and picked up a stack of papers.

"Missing your hat?" the sheriff asked.

"Lost it in a storm a few days back."

"Bad luck, losing your hat," Neil commented as he shut the stove door and adjusted the pot over the hole. "A man usually finds another pretty quick in this country."

"I haven't the money," Martin lied.

Neil grunted he understood, then held up a finger and disappeared through a side door into what looked like a bunkroom. Martin listened to the scrapes and clatters of a trunk being dragged across the floor and opened while fixing his gaze on the window beside the sheriff's desk, aware of the sheriff's scrutiny.

A minute later, Neil returned with a black, flat-brimmed, flat-crowned hat with a tooled leather band.

"Try that," he said, tossing the hat to Martin. "Came off some drifter that got shot a few months back. Looks like he just bought it."

Martin raised an eyebrow at Neil. If losing a hat was bad luck, how much worse was wearing the hat of a man who died shortly after purchasing it? But he was a beggar and tried it on. It fit a little snug but would stretch in time.

"Now," Neil said, easing his weight onto the edge of his desk and crossing his arms. "What did you want to talk about?"

Martin pulled off the hat and set it on his knee, keenly aware of the captain's position between him and the door.

"It's about a couple of your men," Martin said. "They were killed in a shootout with a prisoner six days ago."

"Where?"

"On the banks of the Red, about a hundred miles southeast of here."

"And how do you know about it?"

Moving slowly and deliberately, Martin reached inside his vest and pulled the badges out of his shirt pocket. He laid them on the desk in front of Neil. Then he drew the paper from his jacket pocket.

"I stopped for water one morning. I heard the shots and followed them to where I found your two men. One was dead. The prisoner was killed, and your other man, McGannon, was wounded but still alive. He lived long enough to tell me where to bring those."

"And that was all?" Neil's gaze was piercing. He barely glanced at the badges.

"There was a watch he wanted to be returned to Miss Leighton."

Neil's jaw worked as he looked at the sheriff, who listened without pretense.

"You believe what he's saying, Johnny?"

The sheriff nodded once. "So far."

Neil turned his measuring gaze back to Martin. His right hand perched on a stack of papers. "So you just go around doing errands for dead strangers, is that it?"

Again, Martin's unease deepened. Absently, his hand rested on the brim of the new hat, his right trigger finger stroking the band.

"I knew Dillon McGannon, and I doubt he waxed poetic about Alice Leighton. He wasn't that type. In fact, he wrote her a letter to propose. Never was a man for words or ways." Neil sipped his coffee. "So, there must be some other motive for you coming here."

"I was headed this way."

"Really?" Neil's sarcasm was plain. "Where from?"

"South."

Neil chuckled briefly, straightened, and paced around the desk to stand by the chair on the far side. "I heard about a man from the Hill Country, headed north and running from a noose for killing a ranger. You kind of look like that man's description. Apparently, he is one too quick to use his gun."

Martin felt the blood drain from his face. His throat tightened, and his breath stilled. The image of the dead man pulling him down to Hell returned as the stone walls seemed to close in on him. Bowing his head, he tried to find comfort in knowing he could now sleep.

"Didn't you hear, Neil?" the sheriff asked without looking up from his work.

"Hear what?"

"That *El Muerto* fellow drowned outside of Wichita Falls. Never found his body, but a deputy down there saw him go in trying to save a little girl."

"You don't say." Neil considered Martin again. With renewed hope, Martin met the captain's gaze and never looked away. His path to the door was now clear, but he didn't look at it and didn't consider it. He kept his silence.

Neil scoffed. "Got a poker face, like a professional gambler." He looked down at the badges, and his mouth hardened into a grim line. "I didn't hold much love for either of those boys, but McGannon left Alice Leighton with a child on the way and no ring. For that reason, I'd like to see the man that killed him dead. I don't suppose you'd mind telling me what happened that morning from the beginning."

"I already told you."

"Why don't you tell me more? Like how the prisoner came to have a gun."

"I have no idea ."

"And you came riding in at the end of the fight?"

"That's right."

"And you made sure the other two were dead?"

"I checked them, yes."

"Where were they shot?"

"Hays in the heart and the prisoner in the head. McGannon took two bullets to the chest and died slow."

"And you buried them?"

Martin nodded. "I buried the rangers. I had no shovel and left the prisoner to the buzzards. After I found the letter of execution, I figured it would be fitting."

Neil considered this and smiled. "Guess I'd've done the same thing." He went back to the stove and lifted the pot. "You want some coffee now?"

"If it's all the same to you, I'd rather get some rest."

Curiosity lifted Neil's brows. "It's early yet."

"I'm used to sleeping with the sun."

Neil's eyes narrowed. "Alright, but see that you don't leave town. I want to talk to you in the morning."

Martin nodded and rose from the chair.

"Of course, if you don't stay in town, I might be inclined to think you killed those rangers trying to save your friend Jackson."

Martin glanced down at the dead man's hat.

"You didn't give a name either," Neil said casually, but it was like the warning rattle of a snake.

"Chigger," Martin replied, falling back on a nickname the men of his regiment gave him after his first fight.

Neil considered the name, repeating it twice as though testing the sound. "Heard of a man in the war that went by that name. They said he could slip behind enemy lines and kill Yankees while they slept. You heard of that?"

"A time or two," Martin replied, keeping his tone light despite his skin beginning to crawl at the lawman's recollection.

Neil's expression became haunted as a memory surfaced for him. He shook it off. "We've all done things we'll regret," he said. "Best, it's all left behind us."

Martin nodded in agreement and pulled on the hat.

"Good night, gentlemen."

Stepping into the darkness brought no ease to Martin's nerves. From the end of the street, four men rode side-by-side. They stopped a shopkeeper closing his store. As Martin untied the stallion, he noticed the shopkeeper gesturing in his direction. He mounted up and turned Haze toward the church.

"Hey, you! You, with the Mex nag!"

Haze stopped without Martin's command. Martin stared straight ahead toward the church as the lights from the town reflected off the white headstones of the cemetery.

"We know you killed Jackson, left him to the buzzards."

With a heavy sigh of acceptance, Martin turned his horse sideways to the four riders.

"How do you know?"

"You're the only one to ride away from that camp. Couldn't've faced Jackson in a fair fight if you lived." The one that spoke sat to the right of the middle. The moon glowed at the edge of the horizon and cast a ghostly light over the town. Martin was aware of people beyond the windows and doors, a world away from where he sat. Even Neil and the sheriff stayed inside. Quietly, Martin smiled and shook his head.

"You know, gentlemen, with the way my luck's gone, I was beginning to worry death would never catch up to me." His lips hardened, and the fear stepped back, yielding to the fighting spirit. "I guess it's up to you to tell the devil I'll be along in a minute."

There were four, and Martin was no fool. With the town watching, he opened the ball and shot the speaker before his hand was half-way to his gun. The man to his left went down next, and Martin charged between the last two shooting the one to the right as his gun came to level. The one on the left struggled, his gun hung up in the holster. Without hesitation, Martin put a bullet in his brain.

Haze twitched and pranced as Martin turned him back to the line of bodies sprawled motionless across the hard-packed dirt street. The speaker laid face up, blood pouring from a wound in his throat. He choked and gagged, eyes bulging. Martin stared down at him with a grim sense of satisfaction.

"Rest in peace...if you can," he said without malice as the body stilled, and the head fell to the side.

Holstering his revolver, Martin looked up to find Neil, the sheriff, and the town in general staring in disbelief and horror, but these dead at his feet brought little unrest. He walked Haze up the street, pausing beside the jail.

"You're welcome, Captain." He touched spur to Haze, and the stallion leaped into a dead run. Once out of town, he found the North Star and followed it.

By moonlight, he rode until dawn twilight. Then he found water tucked in a thicket of willows. He was tired, but he had made yet another choice he would pay badly for. Other than to rest Haze, he rode straight through to the border. With little available cover, he hid in dry washes to unsaddle Haze and let him graze.

Though logically, he knew any posse was likely hours behind, Martin felt pressured to move on. He forced himself to rest for Haze's sake. Once Haze ceased grazing and napped, Martin saddled up again and rode out at a steady pace.

The miles fell away, and he kept glancing at his back trail. No column of dust followed him, but the nagging sense of pursuit lingered. He didn't know when he passed out of Texas into the Nations, but the land ahead gave him little hope for water. That night, the waning moon gave too little light, forcing Martin to stop. He didn't sleep. With hunger and thirst nagging him, he leaned against a rock wrapped in a blanket and dozed. He woke repeatedly in the night to Haze's nervous knickers. Coyotes howled in the distance but never came close enough to threaten them. Martin moved closer to the stallion, and Haze lowered his head to be scratched.

"Only you and me, Hazy Boy," he said as he ruffled the stallion's forelock.

Comforted by the contact with his companion, Haze slept, but Martin remained awake agitated by his dulling senses. When the first rays of sun came, he saddled up again, keeping a northern heading. The days and nights blurred, and he lost track of time. There was little chance they could pass through the Nations without attracting attention, but there was also little chance Texas law would follow them through the territory.

Late one evening, he came upon a homestead. Like so many others, it was clean and well-kept. Unlike others, paintings marked the adobe walls. Martin knew little about Indians. What he knew was that with the white-man's ways, these settlers could just as easily know from where he came and why his horse showed signs of hard riding, but he had been two days without fresh water, and without that, Haze could not go on. The well at the center of the yard offered that much. Getting to it was risky.

As lamplight lit the front window, the door opened, and a man stepped out and lit a pipe. He sat down against the wall and smoked quietly with his dog beside him. Through the window, Martin could see and hear a woman's voice as she readied her children for bed. Then she joined the man on the porch. Martin watched and waited until the man and woman also turned in for the night. He waited an hour longer to be sure they slept. Then, through the inky blackness, he led Haze to the well and drew water for him.

In his exhaustion, Martin failed to judge the wind that carried his scent in through the open windows. The dog barked in an unceasing tirade. Turning to mount, Martin froze at the sound of a hammer clicked to full cock.

A voice spoke to him from the shadows of the barn. He shook his head that he didn't understand.

"What do you want, stranger?" the voice asked in clear English.

"Just water for my horse, that's all."

"You too proud to ask for water from a Cherokee?"

"No, sir," Martin tried to ease the nerves that threatened to shake him, but he'd been too long without food.

"On the run?"

Hesitating, Martin nodded.

"What for?"

Keeping his hands in plain sight on the saddle, Martin turned his head, trying to see the man.

"I killed four men in Amarillo," Martin explained.

"Were they white men?"

"I think so."

"Bad men? Or Lawmen?"

"Arlo Jackson's gang."

The man chuckled. Gravel grated under his boots as he walked into the open.

"In that case, take all the water you need. Bad Texas white men don't mean anything to me."

The man came and stood across the well, holding his rifle in both hands.

Hesitantly, Martin reached out and started pulling up the bucket. It took more effort than his body remembered, but finally, the bucket reached the edge, and he poured it into the trough for Haze. Then he dropped the bucket again for himself. Halfway up, the rope slipped, and the bucket dropped back into the water below. Martin gripped the rope again and fought to bring the bucket up. When it reached the edge, he almost lost it again, but the man caught the rope.

"Thanks." Martin uncorked his canteen and pushed it into the bucket. It gave out a long, satisfying gurgle as it filled.

"How long you been riding?"

Martin shrugged. "The moon was four days past full when I left Amarillo. I don't know how many days."

"When last did you eat or sleep?"

Martin lifted the canteen to his lips and drank deep of the cool water. It sent a chill through his body. The night was cool, and the man wore a coat, but the thin slicker Martin wore offered little warmth. The chill overcame him, and he couldn't hide it.

The man looked over at Haze and seemed not to notice the shiver.

"Your horse needs rest. He's been ridden too long. If you want to keep on, I'll trade for him."

"Nothing can replace him." Martin finished filling the canteen and hung it on his saddle.

"I don't have room in the house, but there is space in the barn for you to rest, and my woman has some food. It would be cold, but it would be food."

Martin said nothing as he readied to ride. He turned to gather his reins, and the man stopped him.

"Do it for your horse, friend," he said. "You won't trade. Would you instead run him to his death?"

For seemingly the first time, Martin looked at Haze. The horse stood head down. He'd thinned down some, and though the dog still barked inside, Haze didn't even raise his head in curiosity. Then he studied the man and sensed only friendliness in him. How long had he gone without a friend? Had it only been a few weeks?

Worn past the point of strength or will, Martin relented. "I can pay you for what he eats in work or coin. Whatever you think fair."

The man held up a hand. "We'll worry about that later." He called over his shoulder to the house in his Indian tongue. A light came on, and Martin saw the woman's shadow moving in the kitchen.

"Come." The man gestured for Martin to follow him to the barn. With a gentle touch, Martin woke Haze and led him after the man.

The barn was not big, but it was adequate and efficient, allowing enough room in the stalls for a big draft horse to turn easily. There was an empty stall near the door, and while Martin unsaddled and dried Haze's back, the man forked hay into the manger.

"You come on up to the house when you're ready," the man said before he left.

Martin watched him go, grateful for the kindness shown. He led Haze into the stall and left the horse to sleep or eat as he pleased. Before he made it to the door, the haystack caught his eye. They could wait a few more minutes while he made up his bed. Food would only make it that much harder to do later.

Laying out his bedroll, he dropped into the hay to test the feel and instantly fell into a deep, un-waking sleep.

Refuge

Sunlight seeped through the cracks in the siding when Martin woke. From the gold hew, he guessed it was just past dawn, but as he stepped out into the light, he suffered momentary disorientation.

A child's voice spoke from behind him, making him jump, but his hand stopped short of reaching for a gun. Calmly, he faced the boy, who spoke again, but he shook his head showing he did not understand.

What the boy said then sounded derogatory, and he jabbed his thumb toward the house. When Martin frowned questioningly at him, the boy grabbed his arm and pulled him forward, shouting orders to his two siblings.

Inside, a woman stood at the sideboard, working bread dough. She glanced up when they entered and spoke sharply to the boy. Martin frowned, trying to divine her meaning in her gestures and expression. She repeated herself, this time waving her hand toward the table near the fire. Still groggy, Martin moved to the chair and sank into it. She rewarded him with a curt nod. Then the woman shooed the three children back outside and turned to the fire. She bent and stirred a pot that issued scents that made his stomach rumble.

"Coffee?" she asked, the word heavily accented. It took Martin a moment to realize what she asked. When he did, excitement filled him.

"Yes, please!"

It was hot and fresh. Martin grasped the cup in both hands and huddled around it, soaking up the warmth. If this was all she gave him, he could have felt no less gratitude.

Silence fell over the room, but it was friendly and threatened to draw Martin back to sleep when a man's voice called through the open window. Starting out of a doze, Martin's hand went to his gun, dropping the cup as the door swung open. When he recognized the man from the night before, he felt instant shame as the man, the woman, and the children stared questioningly at him.

"Please forgive me," he pleaded, picking up the cup. He started untying his neckerchief to clean up the spilled coffee, but the woman crouched beside him and stilled his hands by gently touching his.

He was afraid to look into her eyes, afraid of what he would find there, but she spoke gently to him. He didn't know what she said, but the tone told him all he needed to know. Weakened by many sleepless nights and long miles, emotion flooded him, and he let the woman steer him to the table where he covered his face with his hands and fought to control his ragged breathing until the spell passed.

He was distantly aware of them moving about the cabin, speaking to each other as though nothing had happened. When he was ready to join them, the food was ready.

"Here," the man offered him the chair with its back to the fireplace. "You'll be warm, and you can see out all windows." He gestured to encompass the three windows and door.

"Thank you," Martin said, and shifted to the offered place.

"I understand these things," the man said as he slid into the seat at Martin's left. "Have no fear. You're safe here, friend."

A new uneasiness sparked in Martin's brain. "You call me friend very easily."

"Indeed. It's the way the missionaries taught us."

"What missionaries?"

The man thought for a moment. "I believe the whites call them Quakers."

Understanding struck Martin. He had known a Quaker woman who had tended the sick and wounded in a Yankee camp and remembered her ways.

"Please forgive me."

The man waved his hand. "Ah. You have had little reason to trust. You've been a long time running. After all, you slept for nearly two days."

Martin choked off a curse and started out of his chair. The man put a hand on his arm.

"Sit down, friend. Relax. Once you have eaten, you can run off again, but I think it would be foolish to miss my woman's cooking."

The woman spoke to him, and he chuckled. "She doesn't like me bragging about it."

Martin looked up at the woman as she served him. "You understand English?" he asked.

She nodded.

"She doesn't speak it, but she understands it well. So do the children."

The oldest boy, with his stern look, spoke to his father, who rebuked him.

"Uzumati dislikes everything about the whites," the man explained. "Please forgive his rudeness."

Martin regarded the boy, who openly glared at him. "Reckon you got reason," he said.

The man nodded. "He does. His mother died at the hands of bad white men who came here as you have. He was very small, but he remembers."

Understanding cut deep. There were no words fitting for a response.

"Ah, I forgot. I am called Silas. My woman is called Ahyokah, and my sons, Uzumati, Honovi, and Hakan."

Martin nodded to each in turn.

"Shall we call you 'Stranger'?"

He considered giving them the name he had given the lawmen in Amarillo, and then decided against it.

"It's fitting," he said.

"Good." Silas turned to his family, and Martin sat quietly while they prayed.

The food proved to be better than Silas's boast. Martin ate two plates full before stopping himself, afraid he'd become sick from eating too much. The children helped clean up, and though he did not understand their words, Martin understood the gist of what they said. Most of all, he believed he understood the oldest boy, and wished somehow to extend to him some sympathy, but he did not know how.

"Your horse could use much rest," Silas said after filling his coffee cup.

"I know." Martin's gaze drifted to the window where the sunlight steadily faded. "I could use another man to help prepare for winter," Silas continued. "Uzumati is still a boy. He works hard and will fill a man's roll in a year or two, but another man around here would be helpful beyond measure."

Desire for a long rest filled Martin, but along with it came a nagging urge to move on. He lost two days in sleep and didn't know whether the law still tracked him.

Silas patted his arm. "Rest your horse, Stranger. Get your own strength back. Perhaps hiding here a while will let your trail die."

His reasons were valid, and Martin had failed to consider the last one. But as he watched the woman and children do their chores, he worried.

"It's not worth the risk to them," he whispered.

Silas scoffed. "You're the first white man we've seen in nearly two years. No law comes into the Nations, and you could almost pass for one of us if you kept yourself shaved."

Martin ran his hands over the scruff of beard that had taken over his face.

"Hide here, friend. Put your guns away and become peaceful again."

"What makes you think I was before?"

Silas appreciated his candor and smiled, but his expression sobered. "It's the guilt I see in your eyes. I don't know what you did, or why. I don't want to know. Every man deserves a chance to gain God's love. You believe that much, don't you?"

"Never thought much of it," Martin replied.

"You are worthy, friend. I sense that about you."

Ahyokah stepped around the table and put an arm around her husband's shoulders. The boys were climbing into the loft. The oldest held back warily, studying Martin.

Raising his hands in a peaceful gesture, Martin hoped to ease the boy's fears, but it did nothing to win the boy's favor. Glaring, he turned and climbed the ladder, slapping each rung as he went. Martin sighed and stared into the fire.

Silas pushed up from the table. "We'll sit out on the porch a while. You're welcome to join us."

"Thank you, but I believe I'll return to the barn," he said with a shy smile. "I guess I'm not done sleeping."

Silas chuckled and took his pipe down from the mantel. "You can decide in the morning if you'll stay or not."

"Yes, sir, and...thank you."

Silas smiled and nodded in return, then followed Martin out to the porch but said no more, and Martin crossed the yard back to the barn.

It took a while for him to fall asleep. He had to admit the offer was tempting, but he feared that staying here too long would endanger the family. Maybe he could stay a few weeks, let Haze rest, and regain the flesh he'd lost. If trouble followed him, he could move on before the threat involved this family. He would stay, he finally decided, for a little while. When he finally dropped off to sleep, he felt a vague sense of humanness return to that dark void inside him.

The work proved rewarding. In the weeks that followed, fear settled and fell away with each passing day without unwanted visitors. A neighbor stopped on his way to town and spoke with Silas. Martin kept his distance out of concern that word of his presence would spread. He made friends with the two youngest boys, and they began teaching him words, proudly showing him their favorite places to play and things to do. Even the oldest boy took part in this, his strict corrections doing little to make Martin uneasy. With time, his manner seemed less harsh, and he grew more patient and prouder to share his knowledge.

Then one day a rider and wagon appeared on the horizon. They were a mile out when Silas recognized them as old friends and welcomed them with a cry that carried across the open prairie. The rider, a grizzled man in fringed and beaded buckskins, hurried ahead of the wagon and slid his horse to a stop in front of the sod house.

"You old cougar!" The newcomer greeted, wrapping his thick arms around Silas in a bear hug. "How have you been?"

"Very well! Life has been good to us."

Martin hung back as before and watched as the big man, with his age whitened blond hair and laugh lined face, greeted Ahyokah with a gentler hug and each boy with a man's handshake. His attention shifted to the wagon as it rattled into the yard with a scruffy gray dog trotting along beside the front wheel. A woman, young and lithe, guided the horses with a firm hand from the seat. She cast a suspicious glance at Martin as she pulled up beside the trough.

"Lena, come see how much these young 'uns have grown."

She hopped down with the grace of an antelope, and her expression instantly turned friendly as she faced the family. She spoke to them in Cherokee and quickly engaged their attention, but her companion regarded Martin for the first time.

"And who's this?"

"We call him 'Stranger,'" Silas explained. "He has been helping me ready for winter."

The big man offered his hand. "Jack Miller."

Martin took the rough, big hand and returned its powerful grip easily. "Mister Miller."

"Ah!" Miller waved his hand. "No need to be so formal. Few enough people in this country without formal society butting in." He turned his attention to Silas. "Lena and I were on our way west. Wondered if you wanted to come with us."

Silas shook his head. "Sorry, Jack. My place is here."

"Even for a few weeks? I need a skinner."

"I gave that up. You know that."

Miller sighed. "Well, I figured it wouldn't hurt to ask. You were one of the best skinners I ever had working for me."

Silas looked at Martin. "I can't join you, but Stranger here might."

Martin shook his head. "I don't know if I'd be of any use."

But the idea interested Miller. "You know anything about skinning, son?"

"I've skinned a few deer."

"He'll learn quick," Silas put in. "He's picked up enough words of Cherokee to understand us in just a few weeks."

Miller's eyebrows went up. "Well, if you can spare him..."

"Silas..." Martin protested, but the man cut him off with an upraised hand.

"Your work here is done," he said. "Here's a chance for you to move on without riding alone."

Not until then did Martin realize he had become too comfortable here. He knew from the beginning he could not stay forever, but that knowledge had faded in the face of his growing sense of safety.

"If you're sure you don't need me," Martin said, trying to let the idea settle.

"I am sure, and Jack here is a good man to work for."

Martin forced himself to relent. He looked at Miller. "When will you leave?"

"In the morning, if it ain't too much trouble for us to stay here one night."

"No trouble."

As their conversation wandered to other topics, Martin realized the two women eyed him intently. Ahyokah smiled as though knowing a secret. The young woman, Lena, looked less than pleased, and suddenly, Martin felt like a prize bull being considered for stud. Both women smiled as heat rose in his cheeks. Awkwardly, he excused himself and climbed into the wagon, ignoring the warning growl of the dog. A stern word from Lena silenced the bitch, and Martin moved the wagon to the barn. Then he busied himself unhitching the team.

Lena joined him, and they worked without a single spoken word between them. Once they watered the horses and turned them out to pasture, Lena returned to the house. Martin resolutely ignored her and returned to his chores. That was how he stumbled across Uzumati hiding in the loft.

The boy turned his face away, but not before Martin saw the tears. Puzzled, he glanced back down the ladder, considering what other work he could do, but everything was done except for feeding the stock. So, he took up the pitchfork and went to work.

"You know," Martin said lightly. "Hay dust has a bad way of making my eyes water."

The boy looked up with swollen, curious eyes.

"Yeah," Martin went on. "Every time I hide in a loft, my eyes just start pouring."

"Not hay," the boy retorted in English for the first time since they met.

Martin stopped his work and considered the boy, waiting to see if he would offer more.

"Why do people have to leave?" Uzumati asked finally.

"I don't know, son," Martin replied. He leaned the pitchfork against a rafter and sank down beside the boy. "I've asked myself that question many times. I still don't have an answer."

"Then stay. Papa needs you. He just don't know he does."

"Your papa's got you, and that's a lot more than I could ever be for him."

"But I can't work as hard as you."

"You will someday, and then you'll wonder if the work will ever stop."

Uzumati grunted disdainfully. "I already wonder."

Martin chuckled. "Yeah, I guess so."

They were silent then, and Martin considered leaving before the boy asked him another question, but he waited too long.

"Will you ever come back?"

Martin thought about it for a long moment. Too many possibilities lay ahead of him, most bleak and unpromising, but Uzumati needed hope, so he simply said, "I don't know."

"You should. Then you could teach me how to shoot."

Martin's expression darkened, and the boy seemed to shrink from him. Realizing it, Martin ran a hand over his face and recovered his composure.

"Let me tell you something," he said confidentially. "You remember when I came here, how worn out me and my horse were?"

The boy nodded.

"I still ain't real comfortable around people, and I'll have to live with that fear of people, because I killed someone. You understand?"

The boy shook his head, and Martin considered another way of putting it.

"Your papa will teach you a way of living where you'll always have a place, a home. You'll know who you are and who to trust. The way I live, I have none of that. No home, no family, no one to trust. Do you understand now, Little Bear?"

"Yes."

"Good, 'cause I can't think of any other way to explain it." With a grunt, he hauled himself to his feet and offered the boy a hand up. "Now, how about we go over to the house and get some supper? My stomach says it's about ready."

The boy returned to his old serious self and didn't speak another word to him. When morning came, he was nowhere to be found, and Martin did not take it personally. Knowing someone would never return was hard enough to face without watching them leave.

He said goodbye to the family that had warmly welcomed him when he badly needed refuge. He had not known them before, and would never see them again, yet he owed them a debt too great to repay.

As he followed the wagon west, he paused on a low rise to look back at the rising sun and south, toward Texas. How many miles lay between him and Santiago's grave? How many more to his own? The thought chilled him, but he did not shiver. Silently, he bid farewell to the place with a tip of his hat and turned to catch up to the wagon.

Jack Miller chuckled when Martin pulled up beside him.

"Saying your own goodbyes, eh?"

Martin glanced south again, as though at a door slowly closing.

"Say," Miller said a while later. "You got a different name we can call you by? Stranger's just...too telling. If a man goes by that, you know he's running from something."

Martin considered it. Then, from a distant part of his memory, he recalled part of Santiago's story.

"Call me Shiloh," he said, deciding the name was twice fitting.

Miller nodded, pleased. "A place of unity and peace in the Good Book. A good name to start a new life with."

"That's what my great-grandfather thought." He glanced south one last time, then it no longer held his interest, as though the door had shut and locked, never to open again. With that, he tucked the name of Martin Santiago Terraza Mercer away in the back of his mind and tried to think of himself only as "Shiloh," a man with no past.

"We ain't going back," Miller said, as though knowing Martin's decision. "No huntin' left worth having in the east."

The old man's words were definite, and Martin took his word. He looked west and wondered how many days they were from the mountains. He decided it did not matter. For now, he was among friends, and he held fast to his thin hope for the future.

Don't miss out!

Visit the website below and you can sign up to receive emails whenever Tommie Wendall publishes a new book. There's no charge and no obligation.

https://books2read.com/r/B-A-KYTK-MMFGB

BOOKS 2 READ

Connecting independent readers to independent writers.

Did you love *Ghosts of Texas*? Then you should read *Coming Home*[1] by Tommie Wendall!

[2]

After three years of searching, Shiloh finds his family living in central Montana Territory, but the joy of reunion is quickly snuffed out by the lingering rage in his older brother. Uncertain of how to share the secret of his identity with the Mercer family, Shiloh chooses to keep silent until after his brother finds peace.

Cormac Mercer left his boyhood and his twin brother dead on the battlefields of Tennessee and returned with nothing but anger left in him and an ever-present desire to die. Shiloh, a well-known gunfighter, offers an easy and respectable way to end his life and escape the never-ending nightmares.

Redemption seems within reach for both men when a gunfight ends with one family member dead by Shiloh's hand. Knowing his family could never accept him afterward, he flees the ranch to face whatever end Fate may hand him alone.

Read more at https://tommiewendall.com/.

Also by Tommie Wendall

Trail to Black Coulee
Ghosts of Texas

Watch for more at https://tommiewendall.com/.

About the Author

Tommie is a 15-year veteran of civil service working primarily as an emergency medical technician, firefighter and park ranger throughout the western United States. She draws inspiration from the places where she's worked and lived. Her characters grow out of the people she's met along the way in real life and through the pages of local histories.

She currently resides in North Dakota with her dog, two cats, and her best friend, Buck. Together they collect antiques, maintain their vintage vehicles, and enjoy long drives to new places.

Read more at https://tommiewendall.com/.